AVA ANNA ADA

Born in Scotland and now living in London, Ali Millar is an author and journalist. Her debut memoir, *The Last Days*, was released by Penguin Random House to widespread critical acclaim in 2022. *Ava Anna Ada* is her debut novel.

Also by Ali Millar
The Last Days: A Memoir of Faith, Desire and Freedom

AVA ANNA ADA

A Novel

Ali Millar

WHITE RABBIT

First published in Great Britain in 2023 by White Rabbit,
an imprint of The Orion Publishing Group Ltd
Carmelite House, 50 Victoria Embankment
London EC4Y 0DZ
An Hachette UK Company

1 3 5 7 9 10 8 6 4 2

Copyright © Ali Millar 2023

The moral right of Alexandra Millar to be identified as
the author of this work has been asserted in accordance
with the Copyright, Designs and Patents Act of 1988.
All rights reserved. No part of this publication may be
reproduced, stored in a retrieval system, or transmitted
in any form or by any means, electronic, mechanical,
photocopying, recording, or otherwise, without the
prior permission of both the copyright owner and the
above publisher of this book.

All the characters in this book are fictitious, and any resemblance
to actual persons, living or dead, is purely coincidental.

A CIP catalogue record for this book is
available from the British Library.

ISBN (Hardback) 978 1 3996 1349 1
ISBN (Export Trade Paperback) 978 1 3996 1350 7
ISBN (eBook) 978 1 3996 1352 1
ISBN (Audio) 978 1 3996 1353 8

Typeset by Input Data Services Ltd, Bridgwater, Somerset

Printed in Great Britain by Clays Ltd, Elcograf, S.p.A.

www.whiterabbitbooks.co.uk
www.orionbooks.co.uk

For L.F.

As flies to wanton boys are we to the gods.
They kill us for their sport.
– William Shakespeare

WE

Before

Out here on The Spit, where the sea reaches and erodes, sucks and pulls, We watch them come; We will watch them leave; here, where land has passed back and forth so many times no one knows where they are, not England, not Scotland, not Europe, not not Europe; easier just to call it The Spit as people here do; The Spit where there sits or sat a mill, busy at first grinding grains to fine and finer powder, until it became used less, then useless, falling into disrepair, the salt wind corroding into its deep stone walls, no longer a mill then but something else with exposed beams standing hard against the sun setting on this small stretch of land where time runs and ran both forwards and backwards until it too makes no sense at all; stripped of time, nationality and industry, The Spit turned and turns in on itself and so We watched the first day when the interlopers from the city came, lured by the clean air, that particular purity of light so good for photographs, beguiled by the prices; you can get so much for so little; it would have been the mummy who sat all of their long evenings scrolling through house sites when the daddy was at the other side of the sitting room with his headphones on or out running and not drinking as he'd taken to recently, until soon there would be nothing of what drew them to each other left to keep them together; a new home seemed like the best idea, a project! – he'd nodded along; she hadn't been right, not since . . . friends agreed for the best; We watched the day they arrived to view the mill, the boy pointing excitedly into space as they walked around it; this could be my room; calm down, came the reply, the daddy deciding not to notice the ivy clinging to the walls or the potential problem of the bats in the outhouse; that evening, a scant mile west, the men in the village pub laughed; did you see her shoes, her legs, her cheekbones; did you see the child; not all there, I'd bet; some shuddered; wouldn't much fancy buying a place like that; while in the corner teenagers who knew about the things that brushed past faces and lived in the shadows of the old mill stared at their feet and the curious girl took out her phone, looked at The Screen and saw the mummy's enthusiastic location tagging and peered closer to get a better view of her and the child; after, at home under covers, she'd watched her again, scrolling back through time, finding not one child but two on The Screen; months later, as rain eased and webs formed on the hedges, the heat eclipsed The Spit; it's so hot, it's too hot; why won't it just rain; the family returned with an entourage of mover's vans, the daddy leaping out of the car first, the girl in the woods not far behind the house, raising binoculars to her eyes but not caring to focus on the daddy; he wasn't the one who interested her; she was just bird watching after all, the family a distraction, the boy emerging next from the backseat, and finally the mummy, first one leg, then the other, the girl leaning so far forward in the wide branch of the tree she had to quickly steady herself; the daddy striding ahead into the house – she'd seen his type up close too often and was sure she'd meet him sooner than she would his wife; she knew how he'd speak; he'd use words like optimist and survivor, he'd talk about his work the way the ones who had work to talk about did; the rubber-floored corridors, the whitewashed walls and uniforms; he'd not talk about the sharp implements or how they made his heart beat just a little bit faster when he pushed them into someone's flesh, that first weal of blood rising to the surface and how hard he had to fight the urge to put his finger in it and taste it, just the smallest bit; he'd leave that out but she would smell the desire for it on him the way she could smell snow in the air before it fell; she observed how he needed the mummy and the boy to orbit around him no matter how slowly they went; the boy ran into the newly reconstructed house with the mummy following, moving more slowly than she had for weeks, as if already the great relocation was dislocating her, causing her to unwind, caught in this time lapse until she was space incarnate, forgetting how she'd vowed to keep body and mind united, instead ordering plasterers, painters and kitchen fitters in the months before the move, proudly showing off the results on The Screen, as in her room the curious girl watched, taking care never to press the heart button while the mummy's own heart became worn as it tried to grow itself a new skin, hoping to harden and calcify, her mind becoming a raw, hot wire-made thing with ends stripped and exposed, each sparking off the other, the daddy taking care not to see as the girl knew he would, choosing instead to believe in happy new beginnings, refusing to see the shape endings took while the mummy boxed herself up into simpler and simpler equations now she was a thing the daddy no longer needed to solve, and the boy, limpid and beautiful, moved away from them both just as the sister had, neither parent noticing.

None of them, neither the boy nor the curious girl, nor the mummy or the daddy, observed the things We saw as the webs strung between bushes became thicker; We felt it before anyone knew it, the deep sense that far out at sea something was wrong.

PART I

SIGNS AND WONDERS

And we shall play a game of chess,
Pressing lidless eyes and waiting for a knock
upon the door.
– T.S. Eliot

1 | THE DOG

It is the reflection of a basic reality.
— Jean Baudrillard

WEDNESDAY

AVA

The day I first saw Anna, it rained; just like it did on the last day. The between days were days of pure white heat.

So much warmth was unnerving, Mum said.

I'd been in the woods and then I was out walking along the edges of the trees when suddenly, there she was, standing in her garden kicking a dog.

I didn't want her to see me. I'd seen her before through The Screen, but seeing her there, real, in front of me, was different; it made me shy, almost. Her hair looked duller in the damp than it did on The Screen, but her compact body and her long legs were exactly how I expected them to look; her eyes too, when I got closer, were the same shade of green I'd seen staring out at me.

Usually, I am not shy. I am also not *not* shy. If shyness is a spectrum, I'm somewhere in the middle. Things most people care about, like body things, taking-your-clothes-off things, I am not shy about them. I call it fucking when other people call it love. When strangers sit next to me on buses, I can talk to them. Unless I don't want to; then I put my hood up and my headphones on.

What I don't like is people I know. I don't like them talking to me or poking me or trying to feed me or thinking they can get to the bottom of me to examine the root cause of my behaviour. I was shy last year around the doctors when they tried to work out why I was getting smaller and smaller. It was simple enough to me but not to them. They had to complicate it like everyone always does. I didn't know how to talk to them; instead, I sat on my hands. Stared at the white wall. I'm shy around food, which means I'm shy in cafés, restaurants, fast-food outlets, school dinner halls; I am also shy at break times, picnics, morning coffee, afternoon tea; all those times, they make me shy; they make me sick in ways the men in the woods do not.

I knew Anna with her prior experience of people like me would understand this. Maybe that's why it all felt so pressing. Or maybe it was the heat that came later. Maybe I was just bored. It's not like there was much to do on The Spit, other than watch.

I'd met my Wednesday 10 a.m. in the woods. I like him – he tips. I used to meet him at the tennis courts. It made me laugh thinking they were still called that when really no one'd played tennis there for years. Now, weeds broke the tarmac into long cracks, balled lumps of it up at the roots of dandelions and thistles. In the summer, Mum liked to watch old Wimbledon repeats on the TV and wipe her eyes and talk about strawberries and cream and Cliff Richard and what it meant to be British. That's the thing everyone liked to talk about the most. Britishness. What it was, what it wasn't. Who was, who wasn't. No one quite knew what it meant anymore, in The After. Me, I didn't care. So long as they paid well, tipped preferably.

After a while, Wednesday 10 a.m. decided the tennis courts didn't suit him. He kept going soft every time. Said he felt like someone was watching. For some of them, the open space is a good thing, a keeps-them-hard thing; they like the thought of unseen eyes on them. This helps with the tips and the repeat custom, which is important in business.

While everyone else was moaning about the loss of industry

and the lack of opportunity, there I was, doing what I could with what I had. I'm traditional that way. I thought of it as both my insurance policy and my craft. I'd seen the trouble people got themselves in here; there was no way that was happening to me. I was not going to become my mum.

Wednesday 10 a.m. felt safer in the woods – all that nature turns him on; the drawback is, it makes him cry. Afterwards, as he did his belt up, he'd begin to sob. Every single time. A surprising number of them do. They'd sob and they'd heave their shoulders up and down like they'd not cried since they were tiny. They'd ask their heavenly father for forgiveness and they'd say they'd never do it again. I'd nod and tell them of course they won't. Most of the time I think I managed to sound like I believed them. I'd tell them everyone has their needs as I patted their giant baby-like backs and they'd snivel as they hauled at their zips. It worked, every time. After I'd calmed them down and they were nice and pliable I'd say, *The same time next week?* and they'd say, *Yes,* and the following week we'd go through the whole fucking pantomime again.

Before he did his belt up, I'd been facing away from him, pressed up hard against a wide old tree. I'd wrapped my arms around the trunk, the texture of the deep grooves in the bark making me feel safer. The rain had made the bark damp and he'd had me against the trunk for so long that the soft wood had worked its way into me, tiny slivers splintering themselves into my thighs. Later, at home, I pulled out each one carefully; some were easier than others. Some were badly swollen. When I pressed, I could see the pus building under the skin. The pressure it created made those easier to remove. All I had to do was press harder and the splinter almost flew out, pus and blood following. They smarted but didn't hurt too much. I put those ones in a zip-lock bag I marked 'easy' before writing the date on it. The more difficult ones were the ones that had gone deeper. Sometimes I thought my body wanted to hold onto them, a type of souvenir. With the deeper ones there was no pus, very little pain. I'm good with pain; it takes a lot for me to feel things. Those ones I cut out, making small incisions with the pocket-knife I kept next to my bed for emergencies. I am handy that way; it pays to be prepared. I put those in a bag marked 'harder'. Sometimes, just to feel it more, I'd go a little deeper than I needed to, wiping the blood away as I went. I didn't want to make a mess on the sheets. Soon the cuts I'd made would scab over perfectly.

That morning, I pulled up my jeans as he buckled his belt. Tucked my top in. Put on my yellow raincoat.

He did his crying thing. I mothered him. He gave me double what he usually did. I asked him if he was sure – I find it always pays to look grateful and a bit uncertain. He nodded. That's the funny part: it doesn't matter if there's not money for electricity or bread or whatever; there's always money for me. I'm special that way.

It was raining heavily by then. I could hear it on the leaves, but we weren't getting too wet, deep in the woods as we were. I said, *Same time next week?* and he said, *Yes, treasure*, although I knew I wasn't. Treasure's something you find; you're not supposed to pay for it. He went one way, towards the village, and I walked to where the woods thin out towards The Spit. Although it was raining the ground wasn't all that wet, even out of the shelter of the trees; it was as if the rain evaporated by the time it landed. Already the heat was doing strange things.

I could see the sea beyond, still and grey. It was impossible to tell where the sky met the sea because the shades of both bled into each other. The red roof tiles they'd put on the mill cut sharp against it. I liked the contrast. Now Wednesday 10 a.m. wasn't there to distract me, I started thinking about the Value Meter at home – something was wrong with the numbers. They were so low. I needed to talk to Mum about it. Ever since it had been installed our numbers had been pretty steady. Everyone in the village knew someone who'd suddenly had their Value plummet; when that happened, they'd be straight on the Deportation Bus, away to – we didn't really know where. Nothing stayed steady for long, nothing felt stable anymore. I bet in the mill their Value Meter was. Still, the Deportations freed up houses for the migrants from the Sorting Centre, Mum said, or the ones they let stay at least. I tried not to think about it but the more I tried not to, the more it became the only thing I could think about.

    I was standing at the edge of the trees when I saw Anna moving in the garden. I'd never seen her any of the times I'd happened to be walking past, but that morning, there she was. Because I didn't expect to see her and because I don't like unexpected things, I thought of going back into the woods and walking the long way home. I could see she had her head down. I stood for a while, hoping she wouldn't look up. When I saw she was fully absorbed in whatever it was she was doing, I realised this was my opportunity to see her up close. Not close exactly, but closer than she'd ever been on The Screen. Quietly, feeling slightly sick with anticipation, I moved towards her, a little bit closer just to try to see what she was doing, and as I got nearer, I could see she was kicking something over and over with her left leg.

    I should have gone back to the safety of the woods before she saw me. But I thought it would be hard for her to see me through the rain. I have this thing where sometimes I think I'm invisible. This gets me into trouble with people I've met. I ignore them the second time, thinking they won't be able to see me, but of course they can, then they think I'm stranger than I really am. Thinking I was invisible to her was the first mistake I made. I moved even closer to get a better view. My legs were shaking, my heart hammering. She was there in the garden; I was there in the damp and the strange rain. Then I saw what it was she was kicking.

There was a dog on the ground. A huge one with short black hair. It looked slick and shiny lying there, almost like an overgrown seal. Or a pig. It was shivering. It needed a blanket or a hug. It didn't need kicking. It had foam coming out its mouth. So much that big frothy bubbles were collecting there on the flowerbed. I heard it whimper. It needed a vet or a priest. But Anna wasn't interested in giving it what it needed; instead, she was booting it over and over and over and over in the stomach.

One time, when she kicked it, it raised its back leg like a crap defensive weapon, or like it wanted to be tickled, but maybe it was only a reflex because after that its leg flopped back down. When it stopped whimpering, I started to worry it was dead.

Standing there, I realised that by being out in the open I was in a vulnerable situation. I was trapped. If I moved back into the trees, she might see me; if I moved forward, she *would* see me. That's why I stood still. I think I thought if I stayed still for long enough, she might not realise I was there. She was so fixated on kicking the dog; sometimes when people are focused on something, they don't see you coming or going.

When she looked up, I was fucked.

She looked up and her face went pale because she knew I'd seen her kicking the poor dead or dying dog on the wet grass, but still, after about two seconds, she raised her hand and waved at me. That was the first time she surprised me; I should have turned and run.

She shouted to me; the rain sucked the sound out of her words.

I didn't know what to do. It was obvious she'd seen me. I waited another two seconds before I raised my hand. Because I still didn't know what to do, I waved. What's wrong with you? I was shouting to myself in my head. What the fuck are you doing? I was screaming inside. But still I stayed there, waving at her when there was still time to turn and run; I was smiling at her and walking towards her; there she was waving and smiling back at me, almost as if she knew me.

That's how it began, in the rain, with a dog being kicked; that's how it would end too, in the rain, but without the dog.

ANNA

I was in the garden when she came back. It was as normal a Wednesday as any day had been since she'd left, and then I looked up and there she was, standing there, stock still, watching me. I blinked to make her go away. Usually it worked, but when I opened my eyes she was still there; I rubbed them, took my hands away; she was still there. It was clear she was a flesh-and-blood-made fact, there, returned to me.

She was just beyond the fence, out of the shadow of the treeline. It was her coat I noticed first: the yellow one I'd bought her. She'd laughed at it, refused to wear it because it made her look like a kid. I didn't know we still had it.

Something grabbed my throat. I wanted to shout her name, but my voice was stuck. I felt my heart accelerate; for so long I had worried it had stopped and now under my skin it would not stay still as it hammered to escape; would she hear it, from so far over there?

I stopped what I was doing. She had come back for me. Time stretched. I might have been staring at her for seconds; it could have been hours; I had no way of knowing, not with the rain blurring things, with the heat rising from the ground, the air thick and full of the stench of lavender. I'd told Leo I'd made a mistake buying those shrubs in the first place, begged him to take them out, but he'd refused. *It's nature,* he'd said, *we can't interfere,* seeming to forget that we'd put them there in the first place. The smell caught, cloyed, thickened at the back of my throat as she raised her hand and waved.

Tamely, I gestured slowly back at her. Was this how we were doing things now, waving to each other through the rain? It seemed strange, but some things there can be no protocols for.

As she came closer, the rain cleared. She brushed her hair away from her eyes in a way I'd never seen her do before. Maybe she'd learnt it when she was away. Children have a knack of always astonishing you. Some mornings they wake and suddenly seem to be in possession of a new part of themselves. How was I to know what a year away would have done to her?

I could see the light between her legs. They weren't as thin as they used to be. This was a good sign. I'd said to Leo she just needed time to get better, and now I knew I was right. Her hair looked lighter. I saw she'd dyed it, the diffuse sunlight catching different streaks of blonde. I couldn't say I liked it exactly. Hopefully it would fade. Still, it was enough that she was there, walking towards me. Then she smiled, and her smile was all wrong. What had happened to her? It didn't travel up to the edges of her eyes as it used to; it hardly seemed to be a smile at all but a tentative grimace.

As the light cleared, I saw it had played tricks on me as always, this strange, pure country light, bouncing off the changeling's yellow coat. I wanted to slap her. I wanted to bite her. I wanted to hurt her, tear her yellow hair out maybe, but instead I said, my voice breaking into the thickening air, *You couldn't possibly help me, could you? There appears to be something wrong with my dog.*

As she trotted around to the side gate, I bit the insides of my mouth to stop from screaming. I pressed my palms hard against the lids of my eyes in the hope that they would start working again. It was not her in the way it never had been any of the times I'd seen her since. I heard her feet in the mud. I thought, it wouldn't hurt, would it, just to pretend it was her? I could make believe just for an hour. For a morning I could pretend she was back. It wouldn't be a terrible thing. It wouldn't hurt anyone apart from me maybe, after she left.

Therapy, I could call it. I could tell Leo I was working on getting well, and he would be so very pleased to hear that, finally, I was doing something about my condition.

AVA

It was only as I got closer that I realised she moved like a puppet. I'm good with people. Well, maybe not good *with* them, but I'm good at watching them, at seeing how what's happening inside shows itself on the outside.

She was a paper doll with crocodile clips at the joints, the same as the ones we used to make in nursery. She looked like she was pretending to be real. I knew it was important to act like I was taken in by her, so I behaved like I always do: normally.

When she said, *You couldn't possibly help me with my dog, could you?* her cut-glass vowels and long consonants told me what I already knew – she wasn't from here but somewhere better. People round here mumbled, rolled their words into each other, left out letters, as if we were ashamed of the fact that we could speak at all. She was used to being listened to; it showed in her voice.

I didn't know what to do. I'd tried to act like a statue, but it hadn't worked. There I was, in even more danger, with her talking to me and asking me for help. Or maybe she was the one in danger; after all, I am not the right person to ask for any kind of help.

Although I felt sorry for her dog, I didn't want to do anything for it. I don't like dogs. They expect too much of you. The rain kept falling and I kept standing there; we were all getting wet until the three of us were so wet that we couldn't really get much wetter. Something really did need to be done about the dog. That's why I said, *Yes*. I smiled and I said, *Of course I can*, even though that wasn't what I was thinking. *The gate's over there*, she said, gesturing to the side of the house. I made sure to look surprised as if she'd told me something I didn't already know.

I went round the side of the house and opened the gate and walked up to her. She held out her hand to me when I got to her, all long and stiff, and I took it and shook it and it felt weird to touch her clammy skin there in the rain, like we were doing some sort of a deal or something. She didn't squeeze mine back like I did hers.

I'm Anna, she said, and again I acted like it was new information; *Ava,* I said, and she looked at me like she was trying to see through me and then, like she was dreaming, she said, *Oh, so you're just like me, the same backwards as forwards.*

ANNA

When she told me her name, it was a struggle to keep my face passive. After that, when I looked at her, I couldn't meet her eyes; instead, I focused on the middle distance, just over her shoulder. I knew she wouldn't realise I wasn't looking directly at her. How she could look so much like her and be in possession of a name so similar, I didn't know.

We need something to wrap the dog in, I said. *I need to take it to the vet, and I don't want the car getting muddy. It's new, you see.*

I liked the sound of *we* as I said it; the implication that there was a shared thing between us. If there was a task for her, I could legitimately keep her here a bit longer. That's why I said what I did.

The car or the dog? Ava asked. I think she was joking. I laughed, wiping rain and sweat from my forehead, by then my heart was doing a feather dance in my chest, leaping wildly but softly too. *The car,* I said. *We've had the dog for just over a year. She's lovely,* Ava said, *so shiny. It's his food, he gets a special blend,* I said, emphasising the pronoun twice. *Although, it might be the rain. Can you help me carry the plastic? It's in the outhouse.*

We walked over to the outhouse with neither of us saying anything to the other as our feet churned up the lawn Leo had insisted we had laid only a few months ago.

AVA and ANNA

We collected a plastic sheet from the outhouse. It was dark in there, the light battling to come in through small, glassless windows as dust danced in the air.

We'd both been in there before, at different times, for different reasons. The rusted hinges made the door seem heavier than it was. From the outside we pushed, losing traction every time our feet slipped on the mud. It would have been easier to stop but there was nothing else suitable to wrap the dog in.

Finally, the door gave, showering us with dry, peeling paint. It opened easily enough after it was dislodged, squealing as it moved across the moss-eaten flagstone floor.

In the gloom things swooped and brushed against our faces. We didn't dare put up our hands to discover what.

Our skin turned to goosebumps as we found the plastic sheeting. Then more and more things against our cheeks. *Bats*, one of us said; *webs*, said the other.

Together we lifted the plastic sheeting. The damp had hardened it, crumpled as it was; it slipped from our hands as we tried to navigate the darkness and the swooping, clinging, invisible things. We were both relieved when we were outside again, and we each heard the other let out air from our mouths and we smiled. This was the first thing we were complicit in.

AVA

The sheeting was too heavy for me. I could feel my muscles straining under it. But Anna was strong.

She told me to put my side down, so I did. I dropped it in the wet grass, sending showers of water into the air, making my jeans wetter than they already were. It slid and then stopped.

Anna bent down carefully, placing her end silently on the grass. It stayed where she put it.

I peeled back my end and tried to pull it from itself, but it didn't want to come. It took both of us to pull it apart. I held onto the bulk of the plastic as she wrestled parts of it free. I could only see one of the dog's eyes. It lay on its side, half on the grass, half in the flowerbed. I thought it was watching us, but maybe it was just staring at the sky – it was hard to tell. Its side went up and down, slowly, slowly, quickly, quickly. Too quickly, I thought. I didn't know much about dogs, just that they shouldn't breathe like that and if they were, they shouldn't be taking a kicking.

I could see flowers sticking out from under the dog's body, like it had fallen on them and crushed them. Was Anna particularly attached to those ones? Is that why she was kicking it? I wanted to ask but I couldn't. I could smell something like the smell of the stuff Mum used to clean the bathroom. I wanted to ask what it was, but I didn't want to look stupid in front of Anna. I couldn't tell her I didn't know the names of plants or trees, that I'd lived here forever but knew nothing about things that grew on land. I preferred the sea, knew so much more about it than almost anything else.

The unspoken hung between us. She must have known I'd seen her kicking the dog, and I knew she knew I knew, so we were both in as bad a situation as each other. Only, I hadn't been kicking the dog; there was that at least.

Her hair was plastered to the side of her face; she kept wiping strands of it away. I could see small creases at the sides of her eyes. She was older than she let herself look.

What's he called? I said. She kept unfolding the plastic, trying to make it lie flat before she looked up. *Pongo,* she said. I wanted to laugh, but I didn't; instead, I nodded. *We used to have Perdita too, before . . .* she said, and then she trailed off and was looking through me again. I rubbed my arms. My raincoat wasn't lined, my sweat from all the effort was stuck inside it, cooling into colder and colder balls, making tiny rivers run between the hairs on my skin. I shivered but tried to stop so she wouldn't see. *From the film, you know,* she said, and I nodded again like I knew what she was talking about.

Finally, there was enough plastic exposed on the grass to lift the dog onto it.

You take his rear end, she said, like bottom was a dirty word. *I'll take the head.* The flowerbed squelched under my trainers. I'll need new ones after this, I thought. I navigated the dog shit, half concealed in the mud. I stood at my appointed end of the dog but didn't know what to do next. Its legs were so thin I worried I'd snap them if I grabbed too hard. I patted his flank, his hair wet under my hand. He felt warm, maybe too warm. *On the count of three,* she said, then she counted really quickly without actually telling me what I was to do by the time she got to three. She crouched, lifted the top of the dog's head just by his shoulders, his long neck resting on her chest bending up towards her own long neck, bent down towards his. I didn't keep my end of the bargain, I just sort of sat at the arse end of the dog, trying to work out what I was meant to do with it. I thought maybe we needed an air ambulance, something with a winch, but I didn't say that. They don't have ambulances for dogs, do they? Instead, I said, suddenly inspired, *Do you have a sheet?*

She took a while to look up. I didn't expect her to be as slow as she was. These are things that are hard to tell from photos and from screens. You don't get a handle on people's velocity, their natural speech patterns, or the way they really move. When she did look up, she stared over my shoulder again. I realised she was always trying to look through me or past me, like she was hoping to see something else. I wanted her to look at me.

A sheet? What sort of sheet? she said. *Any,* I said. *Just so we could wrap him in it, maybe pull him onto the plastic? Just an idea.*

Of course, yes, good plan, she said, nodding towards the house. *The door's open.*

You want me to go? I said, pointing to my chest; she nodded: *I think it's best if I stay with him,* she said. *The linen cupboard is the first door to the left at the top of the stairs.*

As I walked across the lawn to the front door, I didn't look behind me to check if she was watching me go. I didn't need to because I had the same hot feeling I used to get when the sixth formers watched me walking across the hall at school. That meant her eyes were fixed steadily on my back. I walked slowly, as if unsure where I was going. When I opened the door to the house the first thing I smelt was coffee, the second laundry powder, the third the real smell of the place, a stale, festering, leftover smell all the lilies, candles, banana loaves and sourdoughs couldn't hide; all the things she liked to photograph and carefully exhibit couldn't make it feel or smell any different to how it had. Some things, you can't hide for long.

I already knew what the hall looked like. She was proud of it, always bragging about it on The Screen. Grey flagstones with just the right amount of polish, a large jute rug on the floor, fixed by a non-slip liner underneath, just to keep it in the right place, always. This was a house things behaved well in. The walls were the same colour everyone has. Up the stairs a runner edged with a cream border crawled. Anna pays attention to details, Mum doesn't. But then Anna doesn't work, not really.

I looked to see if their Value Meter was at the side of their door like ours was. The ones in the village had all been installed at the same time; we didn't get a choice where they were put; it was easy for visitors to check your numbers as they arrived, if they wanted to. Of course, theirs wasn't there. It would be somewhere discreet where people couldn't see it.

The house was cold, like damp was seeping out of the walls.

I ran up the stairs making as much noise as possible to scare away anything that might be in the house. There was a feeling about it I didn't like. A feeling that didn't transfer through The Screen.

I'd been there when it was still a mill. I used to take Thursday 3 p.m. there, and Saturday 7, 8 and 9 p.m.s. They said they liked the dark. They didn't mind the feel of the place; I did, so I charged a premium. I was never as good at those appointments as I usually was; it felt like something was watching, and not in the way anyone would want. I thought it would feel different now the walls had been stripped, damp-proofed and plastered, but feelings work themselves into stones and stay there, I guess, because it felt just the same. Anna had moved their stuff in and made it all beautiful, but it was really just as hollow as it had been when the walls stood like bones after the wind whipped the tiles away, hurling them down on the village green. They were the first thing I ever collected, the old roof tiles from the mill. I still have them in their labelled bags in my room. I thought maybe I'd bring them to show Anna one day. We could sit in her brand-new kitchen at the kitchen island and drink tea, I'd lay them out in front of her, and she would be fascinated, and use words like fate, and then we'd laugh about it.

    I turned right at the top of the stairs, thinking it wouldn't hurt to have a quick look around. I opened the first door: it was the boy's room, painted a dark blue just so he didn't forget what he was. There were adhesive glow-in-the-dark stars on the ceiling, the same as I have in my room at home, although mine don't glow anymore. I tried to take them down years ago, but they took the paint with them, so I left them there, unshining, to stare at every night.

    When I used to come here, there were no upper floors, just gaping holes for the sky to stare in through.

    From his window I could see the sea becoming white frothing seahorses now the wind was rising; I watched them break and turn to foam on the shore. I backed out, shut the door and turned right, opening the next door. The room was white, with a thick carpet and long pale-pink curtains at the window. Above the bed was a strange blue painting in a frame; it looked like a person but also not a person. I didn't know much about art, not since they'd stopped lessons at school. *Valueless,* Mum had said.

I'd never seen this room on The Screen. Maybe Anna hadn't finished it or didn't like it. Slightly spooked, I shut the door, turned round and went to the linen cupboard at the other side of the stairs.

There was a tripod standing outside it, with an expensive camera set into it, the kind you need to understand settings for, not the sort you just pointed at things. In the cupboard were rows of carefully stacked white linen sheets, duvet covers, pillowcases, towels and face cloths, with neat labels on the shelves. So much white collected in the one place was dazzling. It made my eyes hurt. I recalled seeing a picture of this scene a while ago – *linen cupboard life goals* people had commented underneath. I didn't know what to choose. All the sheets were white, too white. The white glowed at me as I stood there deliberating. They weren't the right sheets to wrap a shit- and mud-soiled, injured dog in.

I put my hand out to touch them. They were all soft under my fingers. Leaning forward, I sniffed them. Everything smelt different to the way our duvets and towels smell. The towels were especially soft. They'd clearly never been hung on a line to dry. It was then I realised Anna must have a bigger energy quota than Mum does, which meant they must be Higher Value overall. I wondered what band they were in compared to us. Some people, you know they exist, but still, it's a shock to encounter them.

I thought of the cupboard above the boiler in the bathroom at home and what the towels were like there. For ages, it hadn't mattered what colour they were: blue ones, faded ones, green ones, yellow ones, all hastily stuffed in – it was easy in a way when it was like that; it didn't matter what towel I used for what, until Mum started getting obsessed with The Screen the same as everyone else was. Then she put shelves in above the boiler and went to the supermarket and bought white towels that were soft and fluffy for the first few times we used them. She learnt this special way of folding them and posted pictures of them on her own feed. No one commented. Only the women from work followed her; none of them were interested in pictures of shelves and towels, although they did like to post pictures of their kids next to the front door every time it was a new term. The kids, smiling and gap-toothed, the numbers of their houses next to them, their school emblems on their sweatshirts. Kidnapper's paradise. Then the kids would go off to school for lessons about how to stay safe online. Before long the towels were worn and hard, making it difficult for her to fold them the way she'd learnt; instead, she just stuffed them back on the shelves. We could have used one of them for the dog, but not these. These were too perfect to ruin.

    I took a sheet from the shelf marked King-sized Sheets. It felt thick and heavy in a way I didn't know sheets could. I ran back down the stairs and out into the garden where she was leaning over the dog, her cheek on its neck and tears running down her face. This was the first time I realised that nothing about Anna made any sense.

    She looked up at me as I half ran, half sank into the grass towards her. She didn't wipe her eyes or try to hide the fact that she'd been crying. She smiled at me and then she stood up, slowly, like it hurt.

    I held the sheet out to her. *I'm sorry, this was the best I could do,* I said. She took it from me like she didn't understand or care about what I meant and then she stopped. *What are we supposed to do with this?* she said.

I was thinking we could maybe make it into some sort of sling, I said. *Put it on the ground and slide the dog onto it.* I wanted to call the dog by its name but couldn't make myself say Pongo without laughing. Anna nodded. *It might work,* she said. *It's worth a try at least.*

ANNA

I watched Ava disappear into the house. I kept looking up so I wouldn't have to look down at the dog, his single eye open in recrimination.

I tried not to think of that morning. Of the toast burning my fingers as I ran across the kitchen and Leo saying something about the Carbon Meter and how I was burning through electricity like no one's business. I told him it was green – wave or wind or something like that – but he didn't want to listen. He'd have me doing everything by hand if he had his way. Anyway, the Value Meter was fine. As we spoke, Adam covered his ears the way he does when we shout loud and I said, *Sshhhh*, to Leo. I said, *I'll try to ration it better*. And he said, *Please do*. I paused, wanting to talk to him about last night, but he just poured the beans into the grinder and turned it on. It had been making more of a racket recently, struggling with the beans, more ripping them than cutting through them sharply, making the coffee bitter. I kept meaning to buy a new one. The noise was too much for Adam; his hands, only just taken off his ears, flew right back up to them.

I buttered Adam's toast and gave it to him; he sat pointing at it. I leant over, couldn't work out what he was pointing to. *Get me another piece, woman,* he said. Leo sauntered past, glanced down at Adam's plate. *It's far too toasted for him*, he said. *He likes it lightly done. Since when?* I wanted to say, but remembered I was trying to go lightly on Adam. That's what the doctor said was best, *in light of the trauma,* she said, as if he was the only traumatised one. I bit my tongue. Tasted blood. Turned the toaster dial down. Put a new slice in. Put the ruined piece in the compost bin. Adam was shouting by then. *We'll be late,* he said. *We'll be late for school now, won't we? It'll be your fault,* he shrieked into my ear, as I leant over him to give him his new piece of toast. I ruffled his hair, telling him, *No, we won't be late,* knowing as I was saying it that of course we would be late because even on the best of days we always were, and this day wasn't going well. Then Pongo came in and began to do that shaking, wrenching thing dogs do before they're sick. I tried to pull his collar, not realising I'd hadn't put it on yet. In the absence of anything to pull him with, I hit him on the flank to move him towards the utility room, but he did that thing he does where he fixes himself in one position, and with him stuck like that, I couldn't make him move. Leo shouted from the hall that he was off and would be home late and that he loved us, and we shouted back to him that we loved him too, and then the door opened and shut. His car door clicked. I kicked the dog hard in the rump, but it didn't do anything; it just juddered and puked grass and what looked like chewed-up plastic and white foaming bile all over the floor I'd hoped not to have to mop until tomorrow.

I opened the bifold doors where the kitchen and garden were both reflected, the rain making them more mirror than window. I half kicked, half slid the dog out into the garden, closing the doors behind him. Adam watched the whole thing. *My toast,* he said. *You've put too much butter on it.* His fucking toast, I thought. *We'll get you a doughnut on the way,* I said. *Special treat. Then I'll be super late,* he said, pulling his phone out of his pocket. I wish we'd never bought it for him. I'd said to Leo that an eight-year-old has no use for a phone, but he'd said it would be good for him to begin to get a grasp on time. *Get him a watch then,* I said, knowing what he really meant was that we hadn't got a phone for Ada when she'd asked and maybe that had been a contributing factor. *It's not natural,* Leo said, *for them to feel isolated; teenagers are social animals, we all are. He's EIGHT,* I'd repeated, but Leo still came home from work with a brand-new phone in a box the next day. *You can hardly talk,* he'd said. *Not with your job.* I tried to tell him it was work, tried explaining that I needed to be glued to The Screen. But I knew it was pointless.

It'll take two minutes at the drive-through, I said to Adam. *It won't add on any time at all. Well, it will,* he said. *It'll add on two minutes.* I couldn't argue with him on that. I looked out at the dog who'd been sick again in the garden and was half limping, half staggering into the flowerbeds Leo had only just bedded in at the weekend. The dog went crashing onto the lavender behind the new plants. It was a relief to see it fall on them. Maybe it would destroy them and their horrible scent.

Come on, I said to Adam. *Brush your teeth. In fact, no, don't – just this once, though. Don't tell Daddy.*

I picked up my keys, grabbing his coat but forgetting mine as we ran past the coat pegs into the car.

Of course, the road was blocked the way it always was now The Watchers were here. Every week since the news of The Wave broke, more and more of them descended. We'd come here for the peace; they ruined it. They baffled me. *Why don't they just widen the bloody thing?* I'd said to Leo the week before, without thinking. He'd brought his eyebrows together and then I'd known it was futile to talk about roads and things we were trying to move beyond. *We're post-transport now,* he said, his eyes focused on the road ahead. I said, *They still have travel exceptions in place, don't they?* but he didn't say anything back. *Surely it would make sense, in the event of The Wave actually happening, to lift the exceptions,* I said. He shrugged; it wasn't like it affected us.

I kept making mental notes to check the exceptions list – it would be nice to get away somewhere for a bit – but I kept forgetting every morning. A white minibus came towards us, a bit battered, excited faces looking out as it drove by us. Another load of protestors on the way to the Sorting Centre for a day of holding placards and drinking stewed tea. Activists, they called themselves as they stood there.

Look! Adam shouted excitedly from the backseat. In the rear-view mirror I could see him pointing at all the camper vans and caravans lining the side of the road. Even more had arrived overnight. *I know,* I said, trying to make my voice high pitched enough to be convincingly excited. Outside some of the camper vans people were setting their portable chairs up already, striped, checked, floral ones of all sizes in long lines. Hideous. One man was in a cagoule and waders, just sitting looking through covered binoculars. Out at sea, nothing was happening.

When's it coming, Mummy? Adam said. *Oh sweetheart,* I said, *it's not, not really. How do you know, Mummy?* he said. *How can you be so sure?*

I just know, sweetie. When you're a grown-up, you'll know the news gets these things wrong all the time.

The boys at school say – he started. *It doesn't matter what the boys at school say,* I interrupted.

I don't remember it being like this with her. It wasn't ever rushed or frazzled or frantic. There were doughnuts from the drive through flung at her in the backseat, or drop-offs where I stayed in the car and watched her getting smaller and smaller as she walked towards a school she was afraid of. There were only mornings navigating the city streets with her on her scooter, or jumping between the squares on the pavement, trying to avoid waking the lions; there were Wednesday treats at the deli, stopping for caramel brownies for her and thick, viscous coffee for me; there was collecting her from after-school clubs as the haar rolled in and the city's dusk swallowed the buildings, sodium lights painting the pavement orange on the way home, stopping at the park for an extra-special treat. And now, I call doughnuts treats. We learn to lower expectations, regardless of what it is we really want.

Recalling this, I wound the window down as he walked away when I dropped him off. I shouted, *I love you!* but he kept walking; he didn't look round, the way he's learnt not to. If he doesn't see me, then he doesn't cry because if I'm not real to him, then he can last the day. Any reminders of home will tip him over the edge, which it took a while to convince the teachers of, who were so eager for him to have a keepsake or a heart-shaped reminder drawn on his hand.

The details of what happened between dropping him at school and coming home blurred a little when I tried to recall them. That happens sometimes, mostly when I'm stressed. It had been a particularly stressful morning, plus I hadn't had time for coffee. It felt important in the garden, listening to the dog's faint pulse, to remember what took me so long, but the details became confused and indistinct. When I arrived home, there was a brown paper bag next to my handbag on the passenger seat and a takeaway coffee cup in the cup holder. Knowing Leo would go silent or, worse, full-on sanctimonious if he knew I'd had a takeaway coffee, I poured it out onto the drive, threw the cup over the wall at the front of the house. He'd find someone else to blame. The Watchers or protestors or the local kids. I checked my Carbon Meter on my phone, hoping it could help me fill in the blanks, but it was the same as it had been when I left the house; I mustn't have topped it up properly.

It was raining in earnest by then, great heavy sheets of it. I thought about The Watchers and how they sat there in their waders, as if hoping for fish; I thought how simple their lives must be that they could just up and come here and wait for it. The news kept talking about The Wave, as if it was a certainty foretold. Their faith was touching. It hardly seemed probable to me; their jargon-littered science was difficult to grasp. Some people just needed something to focus on, which explained the appeal of The Wave. I could understand that part at least.

In the house I checked the Value Meter as the coffee brewed. It was hovering around where it always did, so I couldn't have done anything wrong when I was out. Or not measurably so, which was the main thing. I was standing by the window with my coffee when I saw the dog lying in the flowerbed. It seemed strange to see him there, until I remembered shutting him out there earlier and him collapsing onto the lavender. He'd hardly moved. I slid the doors open and called, *Pongo!* but he didn't look up. The rain carried the smell of the crumbled, broken, dying lavender over to me and it was then that most of the morning up until that point began to unspool itself in a series of freeze-frames. I couldn't stand the smell of it, never could, not since it happened. And there it was, in my nostrils, the stupid lavender I'd said would be a nice gesture without thinking it through, the way I never thought things through, until all the air was only lavender, the sickly smell of it making time stack in ways it shouldn't, hurling me into and back through the past and shit –

Shit! I'd left the dog there in the garden after it had puked up whatever it had all over the place as I'd taken Adam for doughnuts, waited outside the school gates for him to disappear through the door and then bought coffee and something else in a brown paper bag still on the passenger seat and done whatever else I had on the way home, and now there was the dog, dead, in the garden and, oh shit, Leo would go mad – it wasn't just a dog to him, it was a pedigree, thousands of pounds worth of flesh and bone crumpled in the garden with its puke all over the place and I ran to it and there was shit everywhere at the end of it too and oh my God oh my God oh my God I wanted to yell between kicks but the words were stuck and strangled in my throat and then. There was Ada at the edge of the woods.

My Ada.

She was there, standing, watching me do this thing to the dog she'd never met, the dog we'd bought because we no longer had our daughter, as if lives were equivalences, and look at how well I'd taken care of either of them. Just looking at me, kick, kick, kicking the fucking thing back to life, incanting it to move as Ada came closer, closer, closer. *Help me*, I shouted; *help me*, I commanded, even after I knew it wasn't her, even as the girl went round the side of the house and opened the gate and let herself in and held her hand out to me and said her name was Ava; my heart, my not broken but stopped heart leapt and as it did something I'd forgotten how to feel unravelled and stretched in me. My Ada, my Ava. Does it matter if you aren't her? I sent you into the house for a sheet. I put my head on the dog and wept, not for it, but for you. I put my head on the dog because there was nowhere else soft or nearly warm to put it. My tears ran tracks into my mouth bringing snot with them until my mouth was a mess of salt and saline the way I could swear it already had been earlier that day; when I looked up you – Ada or Ava – were walking back towards me across the garden with a shroud in your hand, and I smiled at you then, I beamed at you, because you have found me.

You have come home.

AVA

I'd waited so long for this. Ever since I first saw her on The Screen in the village pub when I'd never seen anyone like her. Ever since that first night when I went home and looked at her photos and reels on The Screen, scrolling back through to discover she'd had more than one child. Ever since I'd first noticed that, with effort, I could pass for Ada. Ever since I'd watched her videos on repeat, filming myself until I could get all the movements right. Everyone needs a hobby; she was mine.

Then there she was, completely different in real life to the way she was on The Screen. Her captions were always so eloquent, although often just that little bit too long, as if she really liked the sound of her own voice. Everyone on The Screen loved how they sounded, spending all day looking at their reflections as they did. Still, I thought she'd be good in conversation. Instead, she was short and to the point. She really wasn't even all that beautiful close up; there was this coldness to her, like she wanted me there and didn't want me there, which made me want to be there even more.

She's strange. Then again, I'm strange; she brings it out in me. The bit with the name. I didn't mean that to happen. It just came out, and once something's out, it's hard to take back. Especially a name. I couldn't correct my mistake after that. Instead, I let her think I was Ava, a single consonant away from her dead daughter.

When I said it, she didn't even flinch; that's how brittle she is. But then, she'd been making a fortune on the back of her grief for over a year. Some people, they know exactly how to survive.

ANNA and AVA

As soon as we put the sheet on the ground next to the dog the damp below it began to spread through the cotton fibres, staining them first green, then brown. We both knew the sheet would not be usable again.

When we bent down to the dog its one eye looked perhaps more glazed than it had earlier, like a cloud was passing over it from the inside. Maybe it was just the clouds overhead reflected back; the light kept coming in and out as they scudded against the flailing sun, battling to make its way out as the rain began to ease.

We both bent down as if each of us knew what to do, but when we caught each other's eyes, it was obvious neither of us had a clue what to do next. One of us lifted the dog's flank and then we sort of shuffled the sheet under the dog as best we could, and we kept doing this the whole way up the length of the dog's body and then repeating the whole process, over and over. The dog lay still the whole time, as if either transfixed or already beyond the bounds of its own body. We didn't know which.

We worked in silence, each of us intent on our task. We concentrated. Frowning with the effort.

The rain intensified again as the sound of bells came from the village chiming an hour we couldn't identify. We spoke then. One of us said eleven, the other twelve – the specifics didn't seem to matter; we both knew it was already too late.

Eventually, the dog was on the sheet. *One, two, three*, we said, and, now used to working together, we bent at the same time, heaving the dog as far from the ground as we could. One of us was stronger than the other; the dog slid down towards the weaker one's feet, making it even harder to carry. We walked a few paces, slipping over the increasingly uncertain ground as the sea mist rolled in. Then *one, two, three* again, both ends lifting nearly at the same time. This attempt lifted the dog further off the ground; either we were getting better at this or the dog was getting lighter. We repeated this action until we got to the gate where we laid the dog down, opened the gate, got to the car, remembered the keys were still in the house; one of us went back into the house, taking the keys from the hook just to the right of the door; back to the car, we opened the boot, and then *one, two, three*, we heaved the dog in.

Did we check it was still breathing? Probably not. We were so flushed and giddy with our achievement. *Girl power*, one of us said; both of us laughed. The car started, and away we went with the dog in the boot.

AVA

It turned out the sheet was a better idea than I thought it would be. I knew a childhood of watching crap TV with Mum would finally pay off. I'm sure they did something like that on some stupid medical programme once. With a human, though. That's probably where I got the idea from.

I thought once we got to the car Anna wouldn't need me anymore. She was beginning to make my head ache, the way some people do. I'd been trying to think of an excuse to leave the whole time we were carting the dog across the mud. I thought I could suddenly remember an urgent appointment. But nothing much urgent happened to me so my mind was blank on that front. Some people are best observed from far away; being with her emphasised that. I liked her more on The Screen. Plus, I didn't want to get to know her too well. That's when I start to get shy, or mess up, or just plain despise people. It's easier to be interested in an idea. There's a safety in keeping people as a vague shape. Specifics, they always come up short.

When the boot shut, she turned to me and said, *Can you come with me to the vet? I'm not sure I can face it alone.* She looked so little then, in the way Mum sometimes did; I needed to help her. That's what made me say yes. I didn't go with her because I wanted to.

I opened the passenger door and climbed up into the car. There was a brown bag on the seat. *Just move that*, Anna said. *It'll be fine on the floor.*

The car was immaculate, the way I've never seen a car be. Ours was covered in crisp packets, empty juice bottles, CDs out of their cases, and had a strange smell, like a fermenting apple, although it couldn't have been an apple since it had always been there, ever since Mum bought it. None of that for Anna, though. She turned on the ignition and a voice came out saying, *Good morning, Anna, don't drive today, be driven.* I bit the inside of my mouth. I'd seen the adverts for cars like that but didn't know anyone who actually had one. *Can you make it say different things?* I asked. *Yeah,* she said, becoming all animated, and it was then I changed my mind about how she looked and realised how pretty she could be when she was excited. *Listen,* she said. She flicked a switch and the voice became strangely breathless but powerful as it boomed, *Chase the horizon.* Wow, I said. *Really inspirational. This one,* she said, *is my husband's favourite*; she turned the volume up as it said, *Obliterate the horizon!*

Isn't that a bit, well . . . I said. *I know,* she said. *Absolutely fucking bonkers, isn't it?* We both started laughing as the car began to drive itself. *Or this one,* she said: *Anna, let us drive you to the future.* Anyway, she said, *I like driving manually, so I always switch the controls. My husband can never work out how we go through so much fuel.* Then she laughed.

She put the radio on and tasteful classical music came into the car. *This OK?* she said. I nodded, trying not to listen.

The windscreen wipers threw the pooled rain off the window as we drove past the hopeful Watchers on the road. Most of them were sheltering, but some of them, determined to get first sight of The Wave, sat forwards, alert, watching the sea, with golf umbrellas perched at their sides, binoculars held to their eyes. Fucking lunatics.

Do you think they're right about it? I said to Anna. She turned the music down. *Of course not,* she said. *I wouldn't still be here if I did, would I?*

Do you have a travel exception? I asked. Anna turned the radio off then. *More than likely,* she said. *I need to check. Probably. My husband's a doctor; he needs to be mobile.*

I looked out of the window. The rain was making long tracks against it. I tried to guess which raindrop would reach the bottom first, the same as I used to when I was little.

How about you? she said after a pause. I knew she was being polite; we didn't exactly seem like the right Value of people to have one.

Yeah, I said, *I do; my mum doesn't.* I tried to watch her out of the corner of my eye as I said it, to see if she was surprised; if she was, she didn't show it. *My dad's in the States,* I said. *I'm allowed to see him once every five years.*

Oh, that's nice, she said.

Yeah, it is, I said. *I have half-sisters and stuff out there.*

I tried to keep my voice casual, like it wasn't anything special. Taking care to make it sound like I'd seen him in the last decade. I didn't want to talk about him, though, so instead I said, *Do you think they'll evacuate the Sorting Centre?*

Hardly likely, she said. *Unless they evacuate the village; too much of a flight risk. No one wants all of those unsorted people just running around on the loose.* I was sure I saw her shudder. *Would be mayhem. And would cost so much too; hardly worth it. Sinister place, don't you think?*

I didn't tell her what I thought. I just nodded. She was silent after that. She took her left hand off the steering wheel, rubbed her right arm with it. She seemed so much chattier on The Screen. Always replying to people's comments and filming herself and putting up reels. She seemed paler in real life, with nothing much to say. There had to be something more. I told myself I was missing something vital.

Do you mind if I open a window? I said.

No need for a window, Ava, she said, and it sounded like she was almost laughing under her breath. *I can use the climacomfort setting.*

She flicked a switch and cold air began to blow around the car. I wrapped my arms round my body. She didn't notice. We carried on in silence for the rest of the journey.

Having watched her at such a remove for so long, I didn't think she'd be like this.

ANNA

In the car, I decided to try her out for size. I needed to know how much like Ada she could be.

I told her I couldn't face the vet on my own. She smiled at me as she hopped into the car and sat where Ada had. Ada always sat straight-backed; she did too. I tried to stop glancing across at her as I drove. I fixed my eyes on the road.

It is unfortunate that not everyone breathes the same. Ada had this soft, low way of doing it. So low that sometimes I would worry she'd stopped, even when she was awake next to me. I spent years making my hearing sharper, telling it to work harder, the way you have to when they're babies; I tuned into her breath and then, at the end, it changed. It became a ragged, animal thing, a thing she could not properly take. I would hear her struggle for it, and her voice, her beautiful voice, started to come out wrong. Then she was no longer my Ada, not really, just as this Ava was also not my Ada. Ava's breath was another thing. It was loud. It filled the car up until it became a presence of its own, condemning my stupidity. Possibly she had a cold, or hay fever, or her adenoids needed attention. Whatever it was that was wrong with her, it meant her breathing didn't match Ada's the way I needed it to.

I put the radio on, flicked it to a classical station, hoping to block it out.

For a while I couldn't hear her breathe over the music. When she asked me a question and I took my eyes from the road to glance back at her; she was still all wrong. Something about the arrangement of her was off. Her legs were too long. She was too high up in the seat. I thought about stopping the car. Was it possible that I could pull over and tell her to get out? There was nothing plausible I could think of to say. She needed to be shorter – only an inch or two. I like things to be right. It was vital to be precise about this recreation.

Make yourself comfortable, I said to her, hoping she would slide down in the seat. But she didn't. Instead, she leant forwards to the footwell, untied her laces and took her shoes off.

I tried not to look at her then. The car began to smell like pondwater.

She came back up with the brown paper bag in her hands. *This keeps rattling,* she said. *Are you sure it's OK down there?* I kept my eyes on the road. *It's fine, yes,* I said. She dropped the bag. Not taking care to place it down gently, she just let it fall from her hands.

I didn't look at her, but I could still see the blur of her movements. I could smell the damp from her socks mingling with the wet-dog smell coming from the back. She smelt of grass, mud and fresh sweat. Almost sweet; certainly alien. She was a thing that belonged outside, not in here.

At the end, Ada hardly smelt. She stopped sweating in the last year as her body receded back into childhood. As her face hollowed around the skull below, I had the strangest sensation she was becoming simultaneously younger and older. For days, she'd smell of pear drops, the faint acetone on her breath. The first time I smelt it I asked if she'd been eating sweeties, not thinking, and she fixed me with her rounding eyes, knowing the fool her mother was. It was the doctor who told me this was the smell of ketones; with nothing else to feed on, her body was eating itself.

I thought: I will need to get some of those sweets for Ava. She might like them. So many things I'd made myself block out; so many things Ava was making me remember.

Ava lifted her legs, put them and her damp socks on the cream leather seat, flopped them to the side and crossed them at the ankle. She stared out of the window to where The Watchers were. She asked about The Wave. I told her no, I didn't think it would come. She stared out of the window again. I took something from my right pocket. Slid it out, felt the soft rounded edges of it with my thumb before putting it in my mouth. Ava reached under her coat and began to scratch at the top of her shoulder. I could see her hand there, moving around, but I was done with her then. I swallowed, soon forgot about her breathing as the soft blanketing waves of nothingness I'd craved all morning engulfed me.

I turned the radio off and just drove.

AVA

Anna drove like she was two women. Slow and measured to begin with, but at the cliff edge where the road widened, she began to drive like a woman possessed. Going faster and faster until the countryside outside blurred.

The road was slate grey and wet. Surface water sprayed on either side of us as she overtook a bread truck emblazoned with Mother's Pride. The car felt like it might leave the road as she returned to her lane. I gripped the sides of the leather seat, ran each thumb along the stitching there, trying to count every one.

To one side, the fields were brown and wet and empty. I could remember when there were still cows. In the summer when I was little Mum would walk me up to them sometimes, as a treat after dinner. I'd stand on the lowest two bars of the fence so I could see over the top and I'd watch them. One night, we came up just as the sun was setting over the sea; the clouds looked like they were painted on that evening. Red and gold and pink edging towards the horizon. Every once in a while, The Spit looked like a stage set. There was something unreal about it; other times, it was far too real. The cows were making these awful sorrowful sounds, like none I'd heard before or since. I said to Mum, *They're crying. Their babies went to market this morning,* she said. *They'll soon get used to it.* After that, every time she asked if I wanted to see the cows, I said no.

Once the animals went, they put crops in for a while, but nothing grows here now, apart from potatoes some years when the blight's not bad. We're too close to the sea; the strange storms and unpredictable weather patterns make it difficult for farmers. The farmer sold up; now the field is mud, patches of wildflowers for two months of the year. I don't like looking at it or any of the fields here. They might look better once the houses for the Higher Value residents from the Sorting Centre go up, but until then, there's something dismal about the mud.

That day, I found the field the safest thing to look at. To the other side of us was the sea – beautiful, but dangerous. I couldn't let the stillness of it soothe me because before the sea was a steep cliff, with overhanging rocks and precipices, things that would snag clothes, inflict wounds, prolong the fall. There were safety barriers, of course, but those were dented, scratched and, at times, just plain missing, the remaining barriers frequently studded with bouquets in yellowing cellophane, the flowers inside dried out and decaying. There were cards attached to the wrapping, but the writing was all bleached out.

Every time I saw those offerings for the dead, I'd think about how they got there. Where did the cars stop? Where did the people cross the road? Were they not afraid for their own lives? Did grief make them so mad that they didn't care? Is this what happened to Mum when Dad left? Is this what made her begin to fray?

I looked at the fields because there's no point thinking things you don't know the answers to. That's what Mum says – one of the few things she might be right about.

When we got to the vet, Anna pulled on the handbrake and, leaning over me, brushed the top of my knees as she opened the glove compartment and pulled a blister pack of pills from it. Her diamond engagement ring was loose on her finger – it looked heavy; the gold band under the stone was too thin in contrast.

When she looked at me there was something wrong with her eyes. She popped two pills out into her hand, the pack making a crackling sound. She put them in her mouth and swallowed them without any water. I tried not to stare at her. I had no idea how she did that.

Terrible headache, she said as she opened the door.

ANNA

Arriving at the vet's surgery, there were no parking spaces left in the town square; instead, I parked in the bus stop, telling Ava I wouldn't be long.

When I ran into the waiting room, people turned to stare at me. That day, I was faster than I usually am. Some days, I move very slowly; some days, I go very fast. I prefer the rare days where I'm somewhere between the two. When I'm too fast, I feel as though I'm bleeding into my surroundings. I become unsure as to where my edges are. After a while, it is slightly alarming.

I ran to the receptionist and started to speak to her, a torrent of words pouring from me. *There's a queue,* she mouthed from behind her glass enclosure, pointing to the people lined up against the wall. They all continued to stare at me. I'd left my handbag with my mask in the car. *I'm exempt,* I said, but I didn't have a lanyard to prove it.

There was a fat man in the queue. Fat is charitable; morbidly obese is probably more accurate. He was wearing what appeared then to be a normal black mask and was clutching his small, cardboard hamster carrier to his chest, as if worried I might infect it. I moved closer to him and coughed, first in his face and then over the box. He retreated as far back against the wall as he could, pointing to the Threat Level Indicator above his head. From top to bottom it read: Viral Threat, 2; Environmental Threat, 5; Terrorist Threat, 1. I put two fingers up at him. *It's a two,* I said, leaning the top half of my body forward. *Legally, none of us are required to wear masks.* He simply shrugged, or at least I think he did; the detail of his shoulders was hard to work out, covered in fat as they were. Agitated by my proximity, the dog next to him began to bark, pulling at its lead, raising its front paws in the direction of the man's precious cargo. The woman holding the lead pulled on it in an attempt to pull the dog back as the obese man gripped the hamster box so tightly the cardboard crumpled inwards. I thought of the hamster inside, wondering how long it would take for it to nibble its way out.

I joined the end of the queue, slunk my body back against the wall so it looked like I didn't care. Then I saw my dog lying in the flowers and the edge of the sodden grass surrounded by vomit, and both of us heaving it across the garden. The heavy arms on the clock mounted on the opposite wall fell into place, announcing it was already 1.43. I pulled myself from against the wall and went right up to the front of the queue. I rapped on the receptionist's glass; she shook her head, pointing to my mouth where my mask should have been. *My dog needs to see a vet*, I said; I think she sighed. *There's a line,* I heard trickle through the glass. *It's dying*, I said. She widened her eyes, shook her head: *They always are,* she said. *There's a procedure for this.*

I know, I said, and maybe my voice was louder than it was before. *Of course you have your rules,* I said, *but my dog really is dying. It's your fault, you know, if it dies. I tell you what, I'll go out and bring it in here, shall I? And everyone* – I swept my hand round in a grand gesture – *everyone*, I said again, just to emphasise my point, *will know exactly how negligent you are.*

I could see them all looking at me. I knew this was because they all thought I was making a valid point. A cat began to scratch in its carrier. The dog from earlier, still pulled back too hard on its lead, began to howl. I was sure I could hear the hamster chewing, scratching, burrowing. I stared as a small hole became visible in the cardboard box, followed quickly by a sharp yell from the gross man before he dropped it. He bent down with some difficulty, then stood, his face contorting, his bright-red cheeks puffed out. I worried his eyes were in danger of popping from their sockets. As he stood, he lifted a lifeless hamster up in the air. To the casual observer, it might have been sleeping. He moved towards me and, standing in front of me, waved it in my face. *Look what you've done*, he said. *You killed my hamster.* It was then I saw that his mask wasn't a normal innocuous one at all, but instead was inserted with a type of LCD mechanism projecting whatever he said across its surface in a kind of rolling script. I stood transfixed as the glowing letters slowly unspooled the sentence he'd just spoken, repeating *look what you've done you killed my hamster* over the fabric.

They all suddenly seemed like maniacs. They could have been zoo exhibits really, overly concerned with their tiny cheap animals. In an effort to calm down, I tried to observe one thing I could see, one thing I could smell and one thing I could touch like an online therapy course I'd bought for £300 had advised me to do. I went through a phase of investing in these types of courses after we lost Ada, but they never made any difference. It didn't make a difference that day either. My chest still felt as if it was in the grip of a vice.

I looked at him. I shook my head and half opened my mouth, signalling disbelief. Still his mask scrolled: *you killed my hamster you killed my hamster.* It was an inflammatory way of overemphasising a very simple point. The more I thought about it, the more offensive it became. I didn't need that level of abusive behaviour in my life. *Can you turn that off?* I asked. He shook his head.

Turning away from him, I looked at everyone else, throwing my hands up in a dramatic gesture so they knew I was disgusted. I knew someone would side with me; after all, it was deeply disturbing. Who sees a mask like that and thinks buying it is a good idea? But everyone stayed silent, apart from the cat, who, at the scent of the death exuding from the hamster, was scratching furiously at the grille of its cage, banging its head on the top of the carrier as it tried to stand on two legs. No one would raise their eyes from the floor.

I hope you're going to pay for it, the obese man said. *Yeah*, I said, *sure, I'll give you a tenner*, as his mask repeated: *pay for it pay for it pay for it.* I was gripped by a desire to laugh, the way I always am at funerals and road accidents. I wanted to just let it all out. What the fuck did it matter anyway what I did next? So I laughed and I laughed and I laughed and I was still laughing with tears running down my face, streaking my mascara into long black trails, when two things happened almost at the same time: Ada came rushing through the electric doors waving the car keys; I blinked until she was Ava again, and through the door with the illuminated SURGERY sign came the vet, perplexed, with a stethoscope round his thick neck and his secretary trotting in his wake.

AVA

I'd waited in the car for so long that I was shivering. I rubbed my arms to warm myself up. It didn't work. I opened the glove compartment where her pills were. The foil was stamped with a long name I couldn't pronounce and could barely see, the writing was so small. It didn't stop me trying. I watched myself in the mirror as I did, putting on her voice. I looked stupid. I took out a pill. It felt chalky, too large. I thought, if she can do it, so can I. I put it in my mouth; immediately it sucked up all the moisture. I tried to swallow it, but it was stuck to my tongue. I tried again but it still wouldn't move; by the third time I tried it was getting harder to swallow. I'd heard you can only swallow six times in a row before you swallow your own tongue. Something like that. I thought I should be careful; wouldn't want to choke on my tongue.

The pill wouldn't move. I put my hand into my mouth and moved it to my back molars and began to chew it. It tasted bitter, felt like dust. I wanted to be sick. I made myself swallow; I'm good at that.

A short time later, I realised my hands were really interesting. I didn't know how I could have gone so long without knowing this about my hands. I looked at them and the way my fingers stretched away from my body. I looked at the strange webbing between my middle finger and my ring finger. Webbing I'd never seen on anyone else's hands. Webbing that moved down from my ring finger to my pinkie, making my ring finger different lengths on either side. I watched my fingers move. It's strange to look at your hands moving and to know you're controlling them but not thinking about controlling them. It hurt my head to think like that, so I closed my eyes.

I woke suddenly, jolting forward in my seat. I didn't know I'd been sleeping. I didn't know where I was. My hands, my mouth and my feet were all strange things. I heard the sound of a horn. In the rear-view mirror, I saw a bus behind the car, trying to edge out of the bus stop. I reached over to hit the horn, but when I saw which bus it was, I thought better of it. The Deportation Bus always scares me. Somethings, you don't want to see up close.

When I got out of the car my legs didn't move properly. I knew I was in pain, but I couldn't feel it properly; it was a far-away feeling, more an impression than anything else. I realised I was only wearing socks on my feet. I probably had pins and needles, but the pills had numbed my legs. I ran to the bus driver's window. *Move*, he said. *I've a Deportation to be getting on with.* I frowned, went boiling hot, sweat pricking my forehead in the moments before I puked, throwing up all over the double yellow lines, some of it flying up the pole where the dented BUS STOP sign hung. The driver opened his window. *Are you OK?* he said, sounding concerned, which in itself was concerning. Mum said the Deportation Drivers were the worst kind of people. I nodded even though I wasn't. *I need you to move the car,* he said. *It's not mine*, I said, *it's my – it's my mum's.* That felt like the simplest way to describe why I was in the car. *Our dog,* I said, just to help with the continuity, *is ill. She's in the vet's. Well, pet,* he said, *you'll need to get her out of the vet's. I've Approved Passengers to transport.*

I looked behind me at the pavement where there was a line of people waiting, all of them in their Deportation uniform.

Some of them I recognised from school. They weren't the ones I'd have expected to have a Low Human Value. They weren't all the ones who'd sat at the back and messed around. Hard for anyone to find jobs around here, difficult to up your numbers if no one could afford to pay for training; you never could tell who'd be next. *Like playing roulette,* Mum liked to say when I think she meant Russian roulette; I didn't correct her. There was a reason I was doing what I was doing to get the growing stash of cash under my bed. I was never getting on that bus.

Just a second, I said, hearing the sound of his pneumatic doors opening as I walked away; the synthetic, rubberised smell of the hot, trapped air came towards me. I turned back to the car and, glancing over my shoulder, saw them getting on the bus. None of them complaining in their regulation stiff boiler suits. No one said anything. Some of them were clearly from the Sorting Centre, going back to wherever they came from. Mum had plenty of names for them – so did everyone else; I hated the way the villagers spoke about them. At the back, two little brown kids held each other's hands. One of them turned around and looked at me and stuck her little tongue out. When I did it back, she smiled. I think I made her day.

I ran into the surgery and there was Anna standing just inside the doors, laughing and laughing and laughing, like she really was unhinged. The vet was staring at her and so was a red-faced man holding a dead hamster in the air like it was Simba from *The Lion King*. He was wearing a fucking insane mask with *I hope you're going to pay for it* written in moving multi-coloured letters across the front of it, like he was some sort of out-of-shape vigilante; just for background music, a cat in a cage was making the most offensive yowling sound. One of them needed to shut up. I thought about slapping Anna – she seemed hysterical. It worked with Mum sometimes.

I said, *You need to move the car.* Anna looked at me with her eyes weird and glazed. I knew she wasn't really there. She said, *Ada, Ada.* I think that's what she said. Maybe she said, *Ava, Ava,* and I was imagining things; that's the problem with such similar names, makes it hard to tell them apart.

The vet looked at both of us, back and forth like we were a pair of tennis players on Mum's TV. *Is the dog in the car?* he said. We both nodded. *I'll get it,* he said, and then to the receptionist, *If you could sort everyone here out, please. Restore some order!*

The man with the hamster was staring at my feet. He shook his head. *No hope,* I heard him mutter as he put the stiffening thing back into a crumpled box. I stood staring at him. It was impossible not to; his mask was compelling. I saw, *Not with a mother like that,* move along the front of it. I swear it was some sort of shit voodoo. *Not with a mother like that*, it kept on saying. I looked at my socks, which were as dry and hard as board. I saw the brown stains, the imprint of my toes, the green-tinged edges of the brown. We must have both looked so strange to those people; somehow that made me smile. It was as if Anna and I had already achieved something together – we were a team; it didn't matter that she wasn't the same as she was on The Screen; it didn't matter that she was quiet at times; what mattered was that there was something about her I couldn't understand, something far away and wrapped in layers I wanted to unwrap, something that felt both familiar and like something I'd never seen before. Being with her made me feel Higher Value, even if I wasn't. Now I'd felt it, I didn't want it to stop.

AVA and ANNA

The vet told us Pongo was dead when he came to the car with us. He flinched a tiny bit at the new sweet smell coming from the boot as he opened it.

He didn't need to put his hand on the dog's flank to know. He looked, shook his head, then felt the neck where we all knew no pulse was.

He said accident, then post-mortem, and when one of us nodded he told us to drive round the back of the surgery where there was another door. At the door he lifted the dog out, said he'd be in touch. Then he disappeared inside with the dog cradled and stiffening in his large arms.

We both sat there. Still. *Well, that was an adventure,* one of us said, and we both laughed. Once we started, we couldn't stop. *The hamster,* we breathlessly exclaimed; *His mask,* we spluttered.

Our sides began to hurt, our eyes stung.

We didn't see the line we were crossing then. That's the problem with lines; they're impossible to see, until after.

ANNA

Adam was afraid of the rain beating hard against the skylight as I put him to bed that night. It had been so long since we'd heard it that the sound was almost uncanny. It was a relief that he'd had chess club after school. I'd picked him up at five, knowing I only had two hours between then and bedtime to try to conceal the fact of Pongo's absence.

After I dropped Ava at the village green, I packed all of Pongo's things away. I'd mentioned that sometimes I needed someone to watch Adam, even though I was fine leaving him alone. I thought it would be nice to have her around the place, brighten it up a bit. Some company on The Spit wouldn't go amiss either. I gave her my number; she gave me hers. I knew if the toys weren't around, Adam was less likely to notice Pongo wasn't there. He rarely thought about things he couldn't see.
I looked out of the window at the sea as I ground cumin seeds with star anise and cardamom into smaller and smaller pieces. *What a view it'll be*, Leo had said when we first came to see the mill. Like a view was a substantial enough life raft for me, for all of us. I think Leo thought the sea would save me. He was sweet that way.

I'd nodded, though. Made sure I looked happy to go along with it. Maybe he was right, some pretty windows and waves were all I needed; lesser things have saved people. I thought of my mother and her weekly choirs, my father and his tomato plants. Maybe a view would be enough after all. Maybe it was.

Maybe I just didn't know how to appreciate it. All the sea did was make me more restless. In and out, up and down, back and forward; it never stopped moving. I started to envy its freedom.

And then there were the sunsets on the horizon every night when I was doing the dishes. I could never escape from them. Leo liked to take my camera out to capture the sun as it went down over the sea. He would take the tripod and the light meter, setting them up meticulously. After he captured the setting sun, he would get all the photographs blown up, printed off onto canvas, calling it art, and I'd have to put them on the walls. One of them kept falling off, mysteriously; I told him the plaster was too soft, but he kept putting it back up again, so I gave in, let it hang there. I still resented it, though.

The sunsets made me desolate, as if they exacerbated the loneliness that had gnawed its way into me until I was full only of it. I thought then of how I used to love them, but that memory seemed an uncertain thing. I could not be sure of the veracity of it. I used to love the dawn too: those first alarming reds in the sky after shots at a bar between drinks, a night of strangers' bodies too close and too warm, with the bass in your chest reaffirming the fact of your own heartbeat and sweat-slicked chests putting their unfamiliar skin on yours at parties after the afterparty. Dawns where I'd walk home in broken heels with birds announcing the new day from trees in the park. Those dawns, far-away-now dawns, I love – loved. But they were replaced by insomniac dawns, breast-feeding dawns, where my top stank of milk spilt from the breast the baby wasn't feeding at; those were dawns cold enough to kill you. I couldn't warm up all day after; instead, I'd sit, dead-eyed at playgroup, huffing coffee, wishing it was something stronger. I'm still not sure I've thawed out exactly yet. I shivered at the memory.

Leo liked the dawn, especially the dawn chorus. Said it was musical, whereas all I heard were a lot of birds screeching in the hedges. The cacophony so hideously rapturous it made its zealous way through the double-glazed windows, waking me before I was able to face the day. In the spring, he would set his alarm for it. When I asked him if that was necessary, he told me it was so he could be prepared. It was quite an undertaking, seemingly. Soft shoes, wool jumpers, cotton trousers; designed to make him as stealthy as possible. They were varying shades of khaki – more khaki than I knew was possible – so the birds wouldn't see him coming. When he said that, I didn't think it was the right time to ask him if birds do actually see in colour. I'm sure I read something once about their eyes refracting things. I like the idea of them seeing the world as if through a kaleidoscope. It would be more fun that way. Not wanting to ruin his carefully planned sartorial choices, I stayed quiet.

All spring, he left the bed in the dark, pulled on his latest disguise and went into the garden with one earbud in. He had an app feeding back to the Ornithological Preservation Society so they could track the decline of the species based on when they migrated from place to place. It felt a little too late. It also told him the call of each bird, so he could identify which ones he was hearing. *Swifts*, he'd been saying for weeks, *they're late. Well, at least they don't need to worry about being pregnant*, I joked over supper one night. He didn't laugh. He said it was no laughing matter, something about gulf streams and weather systems until I switched off and only heard every third word, but I made sure to nod so it looked like I was keeping up. He doesn't need me to reply all that often anymore. Two days before that first day with Ava, when the swifts arrived he was relieved. *It'll rain later*, he said, and sure enough, two days later it did. He thinks he's some sort of prophet now, divining the seasons.

He said he couldn't get enough of nature. When he said he should have done this years ago, all I could hear was the singular; he never said we anymore. He calls The Spit transcendent, meaning he neglected to remember other dawns, how we met, or going to clubs until closing, gigs, art galleries – things I thought and continued to think more transcendent than, say, flowers. All our past was gone. His head was just swifts, swallows, nesting boxes, flight patterns, murmurations, soft clothes and sunsets; I was nowhere in any of it. I would get the photo albums out sometimes, just to look at how it was; making myself look at her there in them, her tanned legs, the freckles on her nose. She was so alive in those photos that it made it impossible to be true. She is running out of the sea towards me and I am sitting on the sand, the strange angle making her taller than she ever became. Adam is behind her, lugging his little Boogie Board along the sand. Each of them almost looking the same. Leo is not in any of the photos. I didn't notice at the time, but when I flicked through those albums, the familiar trepidation at seeing her face again rising, he seemed a glaring omission.

I wanted him to say sometimes, *Remember when* . . . and then to reel off some stupid thing I'd forgotten. Something about the kids when they were little. Or old friends. But he was in the present tense then, saying it feels good to live in the moment, saying I'm fixated with the past. I needed to move on, he liked to tell me, as if I he didn't realise all I wanted to do was to dig my heels in to make time stop, every passing day taking me further away from when she was here, the increasing distance sending me dizzy. I could not comprehend time properly after her. That it continued to be, after her, was the cruellest trick of all. When someone leaves, the world should also stop.

He became all about conservation. His connection to nature; profound, he said. He used to sit absorbed in album sleeves, then just sat with plant catalogues, putting rings round the ones he wanted. I should have found it endearing but there is something sinister about watching someone you thought you knew turn into someone entirely different. Makes you wonder which part is the act. Does it lie in the before, or the after? Almost every second day, he took huge deliveries of plants with Latin names, he then wrote onto tiny wooden markers he pushed into the soil next to where he'd planted them until the garden seemed to be littered with miniature headstones.

There was more threat than I could have imagined in the garden: snails, slugs, pheasants, foxes. It's a wonder anything grew at all. When the tiny plants arrived as plugs, he hardened them outside, setting his alarm to remind him to bring them back in. Paying more attention to them than he ever did to Ada's or Adam's routines. Although I suppose I was responsible for them, which might have been the problem.

It's Godless here, I said to him once, just to wind him up. I did that sometimes, just to make something happen; on a slow day an argument is as much an excitement as anything else. He pushed his foot down hard on the spade, pushing it further into the clay-tinted ground, wiped his brow. I cupped my glass close to me, cocked my head like I was thinking aloud. *Do you not feel it?* I said. *That nature's in charge more than we are? It's almost as if . . .* – and I made my voice trail away like I was uncertain so he wouldn't think I had thought this over and over on a loop – *there's never been God, just nature acting like a cunt, and us, trying to solve the riddle of storms and weather systems.*

I'm not sure you're making much sense to me, he said, shaking his head and turning back to the spade. I went back into the house to the snug and started talking to people in The Screen, worried he'd take up cold-water swimming next.

After the spices popped, I tipped the onions into the pan where the butter had deepened to just the wrong shade of brown. I told myself it didn't matter, I wasn't going to eat it anyway, but I worried the boys would be able to taste how burnt it had become. The onions browned too quickly, their edges singeing before they softened properly. I poured in sugar next, hoping to sweeten them, followed by spices, then I carefully scraped the vegetables in from the olive-wood chopping board I'd cut them on. I watched the vegetables taking up the colours of the spices as they softened – the kitchen didn't feel as empty then; I could've sworn Ada came in and stole bits of food from the pan as she had when she was a child, but the light was doing the thing the light kept doing that day, jumping and running away from me, pinking and reddening just beyond the periphery of my vision, so I couldn't be exactly sure.

I made a mental note to get my eyes tested.

I poured in coconut milk and popped the curry in the Aga to simmer while I collected Adam. I drove past the news crews and The Watchers. There were more of them every day. I thought for a moment about stopping and talking to the reporters – it could really boost my online presence – but I was already late.

Adam loved the meal. I sat opposite him with a cup of fennel and nettle tea and did things to make him laugh and let him watch old cartoons after dinner and said we could skip bath and teeth, but that made him cry. He said, *I always have a bath at this time, and I always clean my teeth afterwards.* He had a point, he always did. But the day had felt long and stranger than most of the days, so I said, *Well, it won't kill you, not this once,* and then he told me all kinds of things about tooth decay and bacteria in your gums and so I said, *Let's skip the bath and do your teeth,* and this halfway line of re-negotiation seemed to work. I got him into his PJs and into bed and he never once asked about Pongo and I thought I'd won then, but the wind hurled the rain against the window just as he was closing his eyes. Those fucking swifts and the weather systems they brought with them.

With the rain beating against the window, he sat straight up, his eyes wide. I smiled at him, telling him to lie back down as he pulled his knees into his chest. *I want Pongo,* he said. *But Pongo isn't allowed in the bedrooms,* I said. I saw him clench his jaw together in that determined way he has and knew I was done for. *GET ME PONGO!* he shouted. I told him I couldn't and then I told him Pongo was dead because there was no other way to put it. I'd had two glasses of wine, it had been a long day, I was tired; maybe I'd had three; I found it had made me irritable; I just wanted Adam to go to sleep. He wanted comforting, kept crying about the dog, asking what had happened; *Was it because he was sick this morning?* he demanded to know; I told him, *Yes, it was because he was sick. He choked on his own vomit,* I said, adding a flourish.

OK, I said, when he said he was sad and scared and needed to come into our bed, *let me tuck you in.* I picked up my glass and phone with one hand and took his hand with the other. I curled up next to him in our bed, stroking his back in ways I'd nearly forgotten how to, where the hair he was born with still was, patchy but there, feather-like, leftover from his liminal times.

Leo woke us. I put my fingers to my lips to warn him to be quiet as I patted Adam back to sleep. *Where's the fucking dog?* Leo hissed into my ear. I jolted fully awake then. He followed it with, *You've been drinking, haven't you? You know it's only Wednesday.* He added extra weight to Wednesday. I rubbed my eyes while he accused me, as though it was the most reprehensible thing I had done that day.

Pongo, I said, ignoring his accusation. *Yes, Pongo*, he said, *where is he?*

Well, I said, *it's . . .* And then I stopped. Words weren't working; I could speak, but I couldn't make them line up in the right order. I said, *Well, unfortunately. Pongo has. Well, sadly.* I started to laugh; I couldn't help it. Things that were funny were: his concerned face, his barely concealed rage, how much of a disappointment I'd become; it was all exceptionally hilarious. I tried to swallow my laughter and spit the words out in its place, but I couldn't do it; instead, I laughed until he squeezed my arm hard just above my right wrist. I saw his eyes harden. *Will you just shut up, Anna*, he said, his teeth gritted. *Tell me what happened or go back to sleep. You're pissed.*

Pongo is no longer with us, I said.

Leo looked at me. I think he thought I was joking. *What?* he said. *Where is he?*

No, it's not like that, I said. *I was trying to break it gently, but sadly, Pongo is . . . deceased.* I felt it had an elegance to it, sounded less harsh than simply dead. We were going down the stairs and my feet sort of slipped; I fell against him and he said, *How much exactly did you have to drink?* then he said, *I don't understand.* He never understands anything, that's the problem with him: life's some fucking huge mystery. Maybe if he didn't spend all day carving people up, he'd understand things better. I think that's how he likes them, anaesthetised and flat out on the table, about his level of compassion. *Dead*, I said. *The dog is fucking dead.* I was right, I did sound harsh. It might have even echoed off the flagstones as we walked across them, adding an extra dimension to how bad it sounded.

In the kitchen I opened a new bottle, poured myself a fresh glass. I held the bottle up to him, even though I knew he'd shake his head. Sitting at the breakfast bar, I told him all about Pongo. Or most of the story, at least. I stuck to Pongo. I didn't mention Ava. I might have missed out the bit about leaving him in the garden alone for so long too. I was tired by then; he didn't need all the details. I skipped the part about the vet's and the hamster and its obnoxious owner. *What happened to the car?* he said. *I noticed a big dent in it when I got home.*

The thing is, I don't know what happened to the car, which is a bit of a problem. That bit's a sheer blank to add to the other blanks from the morning. The thing about blanks is how odd they are. It's so strange how you can know they're there, but they're made only of the things surrounding them, becoming more what they are not than anything else. I'm used to the way they inhabit a kind of negative space, surrounded by white, but this one was simply a hole, a blackness nearly.

Someone ran into me, I said, improvising. *Not someone, exactly, but a car. A car ran into the back of me.*

He walked over to the fridge; *Forfuckssake,* I heard him roll together. He opened the fridge door; the blue light inside came on. It was too bright. I closed my eyes. I heard the door close. I opened my eyes. He put his zero-alcohol beer down on the worksurface. Rummaged in the drawer for a bottle opener. He looked at me. *At least we should get the dog back on the insurance, after the post-mortem,* he said.

I made myself smile. A big one that showed my teeth. That was so he would know that I thought, yes, brilliant, yes, wasn't that super-handy.

What about Adam? he said with his back to me, leaning his elbows on the worksurface and looking out to sea. *How did he take the news?*

I only just told him, I said. *I hoped he might not notice but he did and* – I began to rub the condensation from my glass, waiting for him to respond, but he just walked out of the room; from the snug, I heard the sound of the projector screen lowering, and the television being switched on – *he took it pretty badly, actually,* I said, raising my voice simply for the satisfaction of no longer keeping it at the steady volume it was meant to be, but all that happened was, in response, the volume of the television increased.

AVA

I saw my Wednesday 7.30 in the woods that evening. Usually, we met down the side of the old working men's club, just outside the village. Sometimes he was fine outside and sometimes we'd go inside, where the crumbling cement from the ceiling had fallen on the plastic seats lining the walls. I think the men were meant to believe they were leather, all the nights they sweated and slid around on them; maybe they did – it's not like many of us on The Spit knew the difference between what was real and what wasn't. Here, if it looks like the thing, it's as good as the thing itself.

I didn't take anyone else there. I didn't like how it was so far away from the rest of the village. I'm safety conscious. Not in a tell-someone-where-you-are-and-what-you're-doing sort of a way. That wouldn't work, not with my job. But I'm always aware of the danger out-of-the-way places present; places where no one would think to look for a body. I hated the thought of going missing, of lying decomposing for weeks or months until some poor dog walker found my skull peeking out of my half-decomposed face. Everywhere I went, I looked for the way out, for the easy getaways; I wasn't lying rotting for anyone. Being that alert all the time, though, it got tiring.

When we were arranging where to meet for the first time, he was the one who suggested the club. He said it was on his way home from work – that's how I knew he didn't work in the village. Only people with official jobs have Permission to Travel

– that's how I knew he was at the hospital or the Sorting Centre or working for the Administration. That's also how I knew he was Higher Value, Top Band even.

It was rare to find one of them. I liked them the best. They paid more and were guaranteed to be discreet. When I gave him a quote, I told him three times what I usually did. Aim high, I thought, he can barter me down, but he didn't even try. I knew then he wasn't only rich, but desperate.

He'd sent me a message earlier that day just after Anna dropped me off, saying could we meet somewhere else after all, and then another one saying somewhere prettier maybe, just confirming what I was beginning to think about him, that possibly he was more artistic or attuned to nature than the others. I sent one back saying what about the woods just by The Spit. It showed as read but he didn't answer. Five minutes later, he replied, **Great! But let's go quite far into the woods**. I replied, **Sure, just by the side of the lake**. We call it a lake for old time's sake; it's more of a swamp now, green and eddying. I should possibly have maybe been more cautious, but I didn't get a bad feeling from him. Some of them, you know what they're going to ask you to do, and you're lucky if they even ask and don't just take what they think they've paid for, and you know you're going to have to be tactical about what you wear for days after until it all fades; but with him, I just knew I would be OK.

Or thought I did, at least.

I was tired by then. I'd spent my whole life being tired. Something about that place, it slowly pulled the life from everyone. All the energy it took for the trees to grow, the weeds to run wild, the grass to turn green before browning, there was nothing left over for the people on The Spit. Everyone was just lethargic, all the time. Mum liked to say I didn't eat enough; I said she ate too much. We'd go round and round like that in our war of attrition, each trying to wear the other away.

That Wednesday, he was there when I arrived. I liked to be early, but he was always there before me; this led me to know he was a precise sort of person. Precise in a way that might get tedious to live with, difficult even. He was just standing there, leaning against the old boat house at the side of the lake. The light was fading, and when he stood up I could see blue dust from the damp paint on his pale brown jumper, his faint outline printed on the boat house.

I laughed at him as I said, *You're like a limpet.* He frowned. *Clingy?* he said. *No,* I said, *not like that. Like their shells.*

I don't know much about limpets, he said. *I barely know anything about the sea.*

Well, I said, feeling stupid the way I always do when I know something someone else doesn't, *they're amazing. You know they have like their own special spot on a rock that they live on. They leave it in search of food as the tide goes out – the incoming tide brings all this food they love, you know, then after they stuff themselves with it they go back to their rock and – here's the amazing thing – it's not as if they return to somewhere in the approximate vicinity; they go back to – wait for it – the exact same spot. And then what happens is even better: their shell wears away over time to take on the shape of the rock and, weirdly, the rock even adapts to their shape. Like they're moulding themselves to each other – proper weird miracle.*

As he looked at me something happened to his face.

Wow, he said, *that's amazing. Why didn't I know that? What else do you know about limpets?*

I suddenly realised I'd been holding my breath for a long time. I do that sometimes and need to let it out all at once. It's not the same as sighing, although people sometimes think it is. He didn't make that mistake.

Well, I said, *I know that if the limpet leaves its spot, which by the way is called a Home Scar, the chances of it dying are, like, immensely high. The odds aren't good for the limpet. The reason is that they always keep a tiny bit of space free on their scar to breathe. A new spot means they can't breathe the same, but sometimes they get lucky and find somewhere new that suits them and the whole erosion/adaption thing happens all over again.*

He looked like he might cry. I didn't have him down as a crier. Please don't cry, please don't cry, please don't cry, I was thinking. Then he said, *I like the coupling of the words.* I nodded because I knew exactly what he meant.

Look, I said, *that's your Home Scar, pointing to the outline of him on the side of the boat house. Where's the rest?* he said. I brushed my hand on his shoulders, feeling the soft, warm wool of his jumper. *There,* I said, as he tried to crane his neck around to look.

He looked funny again as I said, *I don't have all that long, I'm quite tired. Tell you what,* he said, *we can give this a miss. No,* I said, thinking of the money. *I didn't mean not pay you,* he said. *Maybe we could just sit here instead, you know?*

Yeah, I said, *if you're sure. I'm sure,* he said, but then I had a better idea.

I said, *Come on,* grabbing his hand. I started running; he ran after me; we broke twigs as we went. *I think it's just about here,* I said as we reached the clearing, and there it was, the old Way Tree with its spreading branches, so easy to climb. *What the hell?* he said, staring at its branches. *Oh yeah,* I said, *I don't even notice them now, it's just tradition, a thing we do at each solstice. It's really beautiful,* he said, touching some of the bells and ribbons tied to the branches. I didn't tell him I had one of its bells in my pocket, that holding one often made me feel safe. *Give me some help here,* I said, as I began to swing my way up the tree. *You're joking,* he said, *I'm much older than you.* I carried on climbing and shouted, *Old man!* down at him, which made him swing his legs into the tree and clamber his way up to me more quickly than I expected him to be able to.

    I got to my favourite branch and sat back against the trunk. From up there I could see the sea and the setting sun. *Look,* I said, pointing. He sat next to me on the branch and I could feel the warmth of him through his jumper; I could feel his heart and we sat there like that, just watching the sun on the water, like it was the easiest thing in the world; both of us sitting there, neither of us moving, not even when over the sea it went dark.

2 | THE DRESS

It masks and perverts a basic reality.
— Jean Baudrillard

NEXT MONDAY

ANNA

I had been restless ever since the dog died. Everyone on The Screen had been so comforting about him, knowing his passing would likely be a trigger. It wasn't, but I didn't tell them that. Their concern was touching; their outpouring of condolences sweet. I felt loved by them, even though I'd never met any of them. They kept sharing the final picture I posted of Pongo, taken the week before; in it, he sat on the grass, the lavender bushes behind him – I thought it a nice touch. My follower count rose, my engagement percentage skyrocketed. I was back. I thought about running my grief course again, maybe tweaking it even. *How to Survive the Passing of a Beloved Furry Friend*, I could call it. I'd made a fortune the last time I ran the one about children. People on The Screen didn't discriminate, they didn't ask for what qualified you as an expert; so long as you used the right kind of language, had the right look and stayed mostly on brand, they'd buy anything. It was the first real democracy. Meritocracy in action.

As it got warmer, I felt tense, more on edge. The pills weren't working. Nothing was. I couldn't stop thinking about Ava or Ada, both of them looping in my mind. There were things I needed. Things that always worked. I decided that going in search of them a day earlier wouldn't make much difference. Would be beneficial for my mental wellbeing, an act of self-care even. I decided it would be nice for Adam if I asked Ava to look after him; that's why I called her to ask her to babysit, give her some pocket money, help her out a bit.

AVA

Anna was agitated before she left for wherever it was she went. It wasn't like her not to leave a story trail, so I knew she was up to something shady. There was something blanketed about Anna; I couldn't see through her. I wasn't used to people being like this, which maybe explains why I stayed interested in her. She left me a list of instructions as if looking after a kid in a spotless house could be that difficult.

In the snug, I looked over at Adam where he was lying back on the sofa with cushions over his knees like he was barricading himself against me. I smiled at him; he didn't smile back. Instead, he kept changing the channels until he found a disaster movie, then he leant forward and, putting his elbows on the cushions, brought his hands together to rest his chin on his palms, mouthing the dialogue loudly to himself. *You OK?* I asked. *Do you want something to eat?* He nodded. *Yeah, cornflakes and jam,* he said, *in the same bowl. Naw, that's minging,* I told him. He frowned. *What's minging?* His accent was sweet; he took care to sound every letter, the same way his mum did.

Minging, it's like revolting. I enunciated it the way Anna would so he could understand me better. He said, *I see, I like revolting. I find lots of things people would generally describe as revolting actually quite interesting, like the caterpillars outside,* he said, as if I was meant to know what he was talking about. I didn't. When I asked him what he meant he took my hand saying, *Come on,* as he led me out into the garden. They had a sprinkler making an arc across the lawn even though the hosepipe ban had been in place for weeks. Maybe it didn't count as a hosepipe; we didn't have much of a garden, so I didn't know; maybe there was no ban for the Higher Values. He said, *Be careful, you don't want to get wet,* pulling me away by grabbing my T-shirt before the water turned back in our direction. *There's nothing worse than getting wet unexpectedly,* he said. *It feels so surprising.* I like this kid, I thought, he's properly strange.

By the time we got to the hedge at the edge of the garden he was really excited, nearly panting with it. *Look!* he shouted. I didn't know exactly what he wanted me to look at. I looked down at the green hedge, where the leaves were turning brown already. The heat was still a novelty that first summer it arrived; it was strange to see everything so scorched it could have been autumn. There weren't different shades, though. The leaves were only brown, dried and crisp, brittle on the trees and bushes; seeing It happen scared me. We'd spent so long waiting for It to happen that when It did, It was too big to look at. Instead, we said everything looked so autumnal, some even said the leaves were turning early; no one said they were burnt and crying out for water; no one said It's here, although we all knew that what had been future tense for years was now present.

I knew I wasn't meant to be looking at the leaves; to Adam they wouldn't be anything out of the ordinary. *The webs, the webs,* he said. I looked down and saw that the bushes were covered by webs so thick they could have been candyfloss. They weren't like webs I'd seen before; they weren't circular, like a spider's, but long, drifting things, hanging over every surface. I thought of Miss Havisham in the black-and-white film I used to love, with Estella shouting *Boy!* all the time.

He bent down, pointed to under the webs. *Look,* he said.

I bent down to touch one of them; when I raised my finger it stuck to it, but still the remaining web below looked just as thick as it had. Adam was still transfixed; I had the feeling I was missing something, that I wasn't seeing exactly what he wanted me to see. That's the problem sometimes: it's impossible to see something exactly the way someone else does. Not wanting to let him down, I bent my head closer to the webs, worrying some would get in my mouth.

I saw then. Safely blanketed under the webs were hundreds of cream caterpillars, with a black stripe running the length of their backs, black dots to either side. They were as ugly as they were beautiful. In patches they were stacked on top of each other, hundreds of them writhing on a single leaf. As I watched, some of them fell off onto lower branches. There were barely any leaves under the webs. I think the caterpillars had eaten most of them. As I focused on taking in the whole scene, I noticed small black dots – eggs, I supposed; soon there would be even more.

Look at them feeding, he said. *The webs keep them safe from predators. They'll be moths soon. I don't like things with wings, not insects or birds. Or angels. But I like these.* I wanted to tell him angels weren't real, but he had this angelic look to him, plus I didn't know what Anna had said to him about his sister, so I just smiled. *They certainly are very interesting,* I said.

Sometimes, he said, *if you're really lucky, you can find a chrysalis. I have some in my room – I'll show you. I like collecting them.* Seemed like we were kindred spirits after all. He took me by the hand again, beginning to drag me back in the direction of the house, too excited to notice the sprinkler was moving slowly in our direction. As we ran across the lawn the water exploded straight in our faces. I laughed; he cried. Quickly, I stopped laughing, reassuring him he was OK as I wiped his face with the hem of my T-shirt.

In his bedroom he was calm again. He took me to his nature table, where there were some leaves, a few pinecones, some empty snail's shells, a sheep's skull, a tiny bird's skull and a bone he insisted was a whale's vertebrae although I was pretty fucking convinced it wasn't. He told me he'd found it in a field; *A fossil*, he said, his voice high-pitched. I was pretty sure it was a cow's skull, but I told him, *Wow, amazing.* I love city people and how mad they are for nature, the novelty of it, before it becomes the thing that wears you away.

He pulled open a drawer full of pupae. I became even more convinced he wasn't OK. Most kids, they keep their pants and vests in drawers, not fucking pupae. Even though I hate nature, I knew what they were. We had pet caterpillars at school once to teach us the life cycle of a butterfly. The teacher kept insisting they were our pets, but even at the age of six I knew they were the most pointless pets you could think of. They were the furry kind of caterpillars too, the sort that give you a rash. Me and the other kids tried to cuddle them, like you were meant to with a pet, but we ended up covered in red spots. One kid cuddled too hard, squashed the caterpillar to death. There always had to be one person who took everything too far. After that we had to look at them in a glass box, watching them turn into pupae, waiting until they hatched. Half of them didn't. Seemed like maybe they preferred being caterpillars. When I told the other kids that half the pets had died they called my mum into the school; the head teacher said something about *disturbed* and Mum said something about Dad just having left, as if his departure was causing the ill effects. After they hatched, we set them free. The dafter kids cried. I didn't. Although for a while after, every time

I saw a butterfly I wondered if it was one of ours. I didn't know then that most of them only live for less than a month. What a beautiful life, though, just flying around. I'd take that over eighty slow years any time.

The drawer was horrible. He'd clearly been on a mad collecting spree. He told me how the heat had messed up their life cycle; some caterpillars were still being born while others were already metamorphosing, and did I think it was connected to The Wave. He moved fast, this kid; it was hard for me to keep up. I was still thinking about the pets at school and how we got two rabbits after that, although one ate the fur off the other, which was traumatic to say the least, worse than if it had actually eaten the whole thing; instead, it was taunting it, doing the deed slowly. Then I remembered the gerbils Mum bought me when I said I was lonely – my thoughts do that sometimes, they spiral too quickly like I'm thinking everything there is to think all at once; Anna's pills had helped a bit with that. One weekend the smallest gerbil went missing; all I found at the back of the cage was a tiny pile of bones, like a cairn. I took the remaining gerbil, which did look a little bloated, and flushed it down the toilet.

I told Mum they'd both escaped. Every time there was a scratching noise in the house after that it was always *those bloody gerbils* and never the mice or the rats as was more likely since it happened towards the start of her illness when she stopped cleaning. I kept the bones, though. I still look at them sometimes, just to remind myself you can't trust anyone. You never know what they might do to you.

I asked him why he had them all in here, seeing as he didn't like moths. He told me that was the point, wasn't it; if he collected all the pupae, there'd be no moths. *The change in temperature shocks them when they come inside,* he said. *They're dead now. Makes me feel good looking at them.* I didn't know if he was right, but I guessed he'd done his research. He struck me as being thorough. He took his microscope from the shelf – the kind I'd always wanted when I was little – collected slides from a drawer and told me to look. I was happy to look; I like seeing things close up. But when I looked, I saw what he'd done. The first slide had the wings of a fly on it, put carefully in place and covered by a thin layer of glass. The second slide had a moth's wings; the third, torn butterfly wings; the fourth what looked like some kind of flattened intestines but surely not; the fifth, with two clouded-over bird's eyes, dissected and stretched flat. He said, *I make them; aren't they beautiful?* The strange thing was, they kind of were, so long as I didn't think about what was involved.

I thought of the bird I'd seen last week, trapped at the edge of the wood. It had fixed its single remaining eye on me but there was nothing I could do to save it, clamped as it was in metal jaws and bleeding from its empty eye socket. I remembered also finding a bird's body deeper in the woods, its wings torn from it. I'd put these things down to foxes and scavengers, but I couldn't be certain anymore. The sun was coming through the window, turning his hair golden; his big blue eyes were looking at me. He was such a beautiful child; he didn't have it in him, surely. Although I was beginning to learn, it's always the beautiful ones who're the cruellest.

I sat on the bed, tucked my feet up under me and watched him selecting each slide.

Was I overthinking it? He was just a child. He must have found them somewhere and brought them home. No one could hate wings that much. But he'd said he did, and he struck me as a singularly truthful child; ironic given the deceit his mother was prone to, both in real life and on The Screen.

I thought of a test. I told him about the worst thing I'd ever seen, how I'd been with Mum, we'd gone to watch birds in the harbour up the coast and had chips too, just before inflation and drought hit the price of potatoes. We'd sat in the lengthening shadows, Mum watching the birds as I stared at the horizon thinking about Dad. Suddenly she'd started screaming, almost hyperventilating. It was one of her first turns; I wasn't used to them then. She had pointed to the water where a crow had landed on a seagull and was forcing its head down into the sea. The difference in size between the two didn't matter; the crow had pinned the seagull's wings down so it couldn't fly away or shake it off. The crow was craning forward, pushing the gull's head down. The gull kept struggling, coming up to the surface and gulping, but the crow knew exactly what it was doing. I think it must have done it before. It kept on going until the seagull was dead. Then, as if that wasn't bad enough, it took the gull in its claws, flew it into the car park and began to rip the seagull apart, swallowing it in large gulps. It must've been still warm. Mum said we should leave but I needed to watch it. Thick blood spilled on the black tarmac. The crow ate it all, apart from the bones, just like the gerbil. Mum said she felt sick and went to find the public toilets.

A crowd had gathered, excitedly taking photos, but after the crow was finished, they left. I checked no one was watching, picked up the bones and put them in my bag. At home I cleaned some and put them in the drawer with the other ones. The rest I put in a hole I dug next to The Way Tree. I took a bell from the tree's branches and put it in with the bones. Seemed like a nice thing to do.

I only told him about the crow drowning the gull. Not about the bones. Some things about yourself you don't give away.

I saw his eyes. How big his pupils went, how his breathing became faster. *I never thought I'd like a crow,* he said. I knew I was right about this strange little boy, ripping the wings off things, sitting in this immaculate house, staring at his spoils.

ANNA

I left him with Ava. She is such a curious girl.

She was both so much and not nearly enough like Ada that I hadn't been able to unsee her since Wednesday. When I closed my eyes, she was there, just like Ada always had been until I met Ava. In a way, she obscured Ada. After I met Ava, I tried looking at photos of Ada to keep her in my mind's eye but the distance between the girl in the photographs and the one I saw when I shut my eyes was too vast. I didn't know who was who anymore. Ava had both spoilt and awakened something. I felt sick when I thought of her; wanting to see her as much as I never wanted to see her again. After the day with the dog, I thought we would need to move. I thought of putting the mill up for sale – we'd make a killing. Or would have. We wouldn't now, not with The Wave; property prices had plummeted. *The only thing to do,* Leo said when the recession deepened and rumours of The Wave started to swirl, *is to sit it out, otherwise our Value Rating will never recover.* We were stuck here. After I met her, I decided I'd drive everywhere, completely avoid the village, which wouldn't be such a hardship, but Ava lurked in the woods; she was never not there. There was no point in trying to avoid her; better then to embrace the potential of her existence.

I thought all these things as I dialled her number. I needed her to come and sit with Adam. He was used to me leaving him on a Tuesday, but two consecutive days felt like a stretch, and there was the risk he'd say something to Leo, which didn't work out well the last time. As I dialled, I felt a growing revulsion at the back of my throat. Even then, I wanted her as much as I did not want her. Still, I let the phone ring and she answered in her funny hard voice, quickly adapting it when she realised it was me.

In the car I unbuttoned my blouse, the bruises on the top of my right breast had faded to an ugly brown. I leant forward; I thought I could still see teeth marks, but more than likely it was where I'd scratched. I wound down the window to let the air in; none came. That whole week was airless in a way I'd never known. No breeze came off the sea; the leaves on trees, stationary. The heat became viscous, a thing we stuck to and could barely move around; as it swelled there was only room for it, not us. I was certain it did not want us there. I tried to say this to Leo; instead, it came out as, *It's hot. Sure is,* he replied as he walked with his back to me from the kitchen into the utility and I stood polishing a glass for longer than necessary.

Some nights I dreamt of the heat. Other nights, of Ada. Others, Ava. Others, both, until they blurred into each other and I was no longer sure who I was dreaming about; I'd wake with the sheets stuck to me, sweat running down my back. In the bathroom I'd put my wrists under the cold tap until my teeth chattered. It was supposed to help. It didn't. I took different pills to stay awake; easier that than to dream the muddling dreams of the two of them, one of them, the three of us.

I heard The Watchers through the open window; they formed a ceaseless background chatter. It reminded me of the city. After Ada went, I used to go up to the roof in the middle of the night. I'd sit out there on the flat part, light pollution creating a night-long dawn. Sitting there, I'd hear the city, a noise not made from traffic or planes; not a human-made noise but something else; the city pulsed, becoming its own living organism. It comforted me. Here, I used to go in the garden hoping for similar, but all I heard was the scream of foxes and the cries of owls punctuating the awful silence, and between 2 a.m. and 4 a.m. not a single sound. If blackness had a sound, it would be the noise of that silence.

I buttoned up my shirt. It was pointless, really, to keep doing it. I wanted him to notice but he didn't notice anything. I could put a thing right in front of him and he'd refuse to see it. At first, I thought he'd say, *Where did you get those bruises?* or *ANNA –* he'd raise his voice, which is all I wanted him to do,to get some sort of response out of him. *ANNA,* I needed him to scream, *who did that to you?* or, *ANNA, YOU'VE DONE IT AGAIN.* But no. I got undressed right in front of him and he didn't notice, time after time. I wondered which version of me he saw. How far back he wanted to remember. Because I knew he didn't want to see this incarnation.

I went back for more and more bruises, but he just put his pyjamas on – even in the heat – took his shirt through to the laundry basket, balled his socks together so they stayed in a pair. I would lie there, naked, with the sheet off, thinking this time he will notice, but most of the time he would come back from brushing his teeth and say, *I'll take the bed in the spare room; it's too hot to sleep together.*

Maybe this time I will ask to be covered in them, I thought. Maybe I will ask to be whipped and lacerated, and with bleeding sores I will stand in front of him, pull the curtains wide open and let the sun eat its way into the room; I will stand there, lit all over, and he will see what has been done to me and then he will say something.

After Ada, he told me he was building a wall – a means to

protect himself, he called it. I could not live with a wall. I knew I would scream this at him one day.

I put the car into drive and went in search of fresh wounds.

When he first started his programme of self-improvement, his slow quieting, I thought he was becoming someone he was not. I saw how he no longer put records on in the evening like he used to when he'd sit smoking weed, listening for hours, covered in sound and smoke. I watched as he stopped agreeing to go to galleries, opening nights. Depression, I thought; I knew the signs. It was as if he was muting himself, but I was wrong. He wasn't. He was just reverting to who he'd always been; the person he hadn't let me see when we'd first met. I'd been so busy planning places to go, filling up all our time, I'd been so busy that I hadn't realised he was full up of me and just did all the things I did because that's what he thought I wanted. What a fucking mess.

After Ada, I stopped. What use was art? Music? Food? Sex even? The temporary reprieve of forgetting they brought only made the times I remembered her more terrible. What I needed was to be numb, that way I could know what had happened but feel nothing about it. This was the state that would keep me safe. Pills worked, powder didn't. Although being high was preferable to being level. Above or below; fast or slow: the only things I could stand now. But once a week, I needed to be hurt just to check I could still feel. It was this pain that reminded me I was still human and not machine, as I often feared I was becoming.

One of The Watchers yelled *slow down* at me as I sped past them. I thought about stopping the car to have a go at them like I had last week when I'd accidentally clipped a chair set too far out into the road, but I remembered how they'd threatened to film me and, with a job like mine, I had to be careful.

As Leo returned to himself, finally revealing how much of a stranger he was to me, I saw how little of him appealed to me and how little of me appealed to him. All these years, we had nothing in common without even noticing, and now, there we were, stuck on this piece of land with Adam between us; how could we keep him safe with our track record? How could I expect Leo to do the same, when I didn't even know who he was?

I stopped the car. Rummaged in my bag for some cash. Since the bloody dog had eaten all my supplies, I needed to stock up, but I'd been in such a hurry I'd forgotten to get any out. I couldn't risk using the card now Leo forensically checked every statement. I'd have to just stick to what I was there for, come back another time for the powder.

AVA

After we'd been in his room, he showed me how to mix jam into his cornflakes; he was excited because it made his milk pink. I remembered what it was like to be little and how easy it was to get your kicks. Without thinking, I put the spoon down on the white work surface. Adam picked it up right away, saying, *You need to be careful, it'll stain*. I wasn't used to having to think like this. The work surface was cold, made from marble or stone – expensive, for sure; probably also temperamental. Who puts something like that in a kitchen? I looked under the sink for something to clean it with; Adam said to look in the pantry.

I remembered the pantry from the photos Anna had posted when the kitchen was installed. Even then, I wasn't prepared for the size of it; it was way bigger than our kitchen. Shelves stretched from floor to ceiling with rows of neatly labelled, identical glass jars sitting on them. How much time did she have on her hands? Other people kept stuff in packets, but not Anna. Only glass jars were good enough for her. When I ran my finger over the cool glass, no dust stuck to it; she must've spent hours dusting the jars. Everything about this house was designed to be seen or shared on The Screen. Everything was a money-making opportunity. Maybe it was a mistake to have been so impressed by the lives I watched through The Screen, night after night. I watched but didn't join in because I had nothing that looked like theirs. No one here had anything much to show off. We didn't have any digital currency, nothing to trade in. No one would want to look at us. Anna, though, she had her pantry and her project, her glass jars and imported floor tiles, her crazy-thread-count linen, and all of it carefully chronicled and catalogued for everyone to see. For anyone to envy.

I stood in the pantry, unable to find anything to clean the mess with, until Adam came in telling me, *They're all down here, out of the way of the perishables.* I opened the lid of the large storage container, chose a cleaning spray that didn't have a warning about being used on granite, or marble, or steel, that didn't have disclaimers about inhalation or what they might do to your eyes. There were some seriously dangerous products in there. Made you think.

As I was walking out of the pantry, I saw their Value Meter, high up on the wall. I had to stand on tiptoes to read it. I couldn't believe what I saw. Five figures. Who has five fucking figures on their meter? They must have been on a combined plan, but still, five figures. They'd never need to be afraid or worry about anything. No wonder Anna couldn't grasp the idea of The Wave; the news mustn't have meant much to her. Some people's consciousness, it's hard to dent. For a moment, I didn't care about how awful it must've been to clean the house or to make it perfect, I just wanted that level of security.

Although I cleaned the stain, you could still see the outline. I bet Anna had some kind of ultraviolet torch she'd use when she got home, just to check there were no foreign substances lurking in the kitchen. Pathological, some people would call her. Adam was in the snug by that time; I could hear the disaster film he'd been watching earlier with his little sing-song voice just a beat behind, repeating the dialogue.

I took the washing Anna had asked me to sort and began to fold it. It had a kind of double freshness to it. Again, I realised that rich people's washing even had a different smell. I folded maybe five things until I began to worry I was doing it wrong. I thought about some of the people I saw on The Screen, the ones telling everyone what to wear – they had a special way of folding tops; not the way I was doing it, for sure. I was folding them into four, matching sleeve to sleeve, then folding across the middle. It looked wrong. I checked my phone and practised doing it the way they told me to, laying it flat on the kitchen island, pulling the sides in until the sleeves met, then folding the bottom up towards the neck. It looked more Anna.

Near the bottom of the basket were some of her dresses. I held one up to me. It was grey with thin straps, the material thick and soft. I check the label to find out what kind of material it was – silk, it said. I remembered reading about silkworms at school, something about how they made one of the strongest materials, but what I was holding didn't feel strong. I wanted to put it on. I held it up against me, saw how well it would fit me. I moved from side to side, pressing it over my stomach; is this how it felt, I wanted to know, to be rich, to have money to spend on dresses you'd hardly ever wear? I didn't know how to fold it, so I put it back in the basket, thinking she would probably take it upstairs to hang. Maybe I should take it up, I thought, so I went through to the snug with the basket under my arm. Adam smiled at me. *You look like my mum,* he said. *You think?* I asked, surprised, thinking I knew who I looked like. *Yeah, I thought it was her,* he said, but he was glued to his film again, so maybe he wasn't paying all that much attention.

ANNA

Having got what I came for, I left The Hill. It hurt to turn the steering wheel – already both my wrists were purple. The sun was going down over the sea; Leo would have been sad to miss it. He liked to talk about being shut inside all day and what a hardship it was, said that's why he loved being outside so much. Easier to miss what you don't have, I thought, and there it was, the thought that tripped the wire. Most days, there was always one, just waiting to ambush me.

    I willed myself to keep my eyes on the road. I needed to bring Ada back into focus. I couldn't do it, not with Ava in my head now. They blurred there. I tried to concentrate. My chest hurt; it was impossible to breathe deeply enough. I pulled myself up in my seat so I could see in the rear-view mirror; my buttons were open, my skin purpling in the gathering dark. My heart leaping, slowing, pounding; my heart, a mess. Everything hurt and hurt and hurt. I could hardly grip the steering wheel. They had hurt me more than I meant them to. It had hurt more than I wanted it to. The pain brought me back to you, my darling, but too close, right back to the day it happened. All I wanted was to not feel; I'd done the wrong thing going in search of such extreme bruises; I was back with you, I was holding your head, I was rubbing your feet, I was head bent over you, refusing to cry; I was bruised outside but worse inside, I was where I could not let myself be because every time I was back with you, I had to leave; I would rather never be where you were than leave you there; there is a world with you in it and it is the only one I want to exist in; everywhere else you are absent and it is an atmosphere so alien I cannot breathe in it; there is no oxygen where you are not; every time I leave you, I know I am not strong enough to do it again; rather eternal numbness than the searing heat I felt there behind the wheel as I drove away from The Hill. I knew this was the last time I could let myself feel pain; I was not strong enough to find you and then leave you again.

Hearing a noise under the passenger seat, I glanced across; there you were. You smiled at me. It was your smile this time, not Ava's imitation. I breathed out. I laughed and could not stop. The relief of it. You were there. You drew your knees up to your chest and hugged your arms around them. How could I have forgotten this was what you did? How could I have mistaken her for you? You saw my bruises; you asked if I was OK. I told you of course I was. You laughed. *You're never OK*, you said; *No, I am*, I said, *I am, I am, I am*; I kept repeating it because you were there and so was I. *But your skin,* you said; *Ignore it,* I said. *Just a silly mistake.* You turned the radio up loud, too loud, the songs I used to call stupid pop songs, and haven't been able to listen to since you left, filling the car. You started to sing, to fidget, to play with the controls. You craned your neck in the direction of the sea where the sun was red sinking into it. *Dad would love that,* I said; you laughed. *I've missed your bad jokes,* you said. You were so alive. You were so alive. You. Were. So. Alive. How dare you be past tense. I get it wrong all the time. I stopped the car, nearly spinning us off the thin track. *Careful,* you shouted, returning to the present tense. I opened the door, threw up bile on the brown grass. Blinked, rubbed my eyes; you couldn't be there. I looked over to you; you were still where you couldn't be. You were still there, you were opening the door, you were saying you would open the gate at the other side of the cattle grid; you were walking across it, your calves taut, your shorts too short; I was thinking I need to take you shopping – your clothes were nearly two years too small. You were walking across the grid with your straight back walking away from me and I was flicking the headlights on as you were opening the gate and you opened it and waved as I drove past. You were waving. Why were you waving? Why were you waving goodbye? Not goodbye. I was slowing, I was stopping. I stopped. You were still waving. I was opening the car door and you were still waving. I wanted you to stop waving. You were not allowed to say goodbye. I was shouting then, I was shouting, *Get in*, but you were not getting in, you were waving, and the air was filling with the sound of your music; I was screaming, then I was screaming ADAADAADAADAADA but you weren't doing anything, you wouldn't move. I got out of the car and I was running towards you as you disappeared, leaving only the night behind you.

    Slowly, I walked back to the car. Turned the radio off and sat in silence as I first swallowed two pills, then crushed three more hard between my teeth. No amount of them could be enough or too much. I waited for them to work. They didn't. I remembered older tricks. I rolled my sleeve up, sank my teeth into my arm, but not hard enough to break the flesh. It didn't do what I needed it to. The second time, I bit down as hard as I could, my teeth through my skin, tasting my weak blood, feeling nothing at all.

AVA

I'd nearly finished emptying the dishwasher when I heard him screaming. I ran into the snug, asking him what was wrong. He was screaming so badly, he barely registered that I was there. I took him tightly by the shoulders – this sometimes helped with Mum; it didn't help him.

He didn't realise I was there; even though I was repeating that he was OK, he just kept screaming and I kept patting his hair, until eventually he registered that I was with him. He continued to sob and gulp for a while, but at least he was quieter.

Look, he said, holding his leg out as he stopped sobbing. There was a scab, half on, half off. *It's only a scab,* I told him. *You shouldn't have picked it, it's not ready to come off.* It was oozing blood at the edges. *I think I'm crying because I'm still sad about Pongo,* he said, which was sweet, but obviously an excuse. I told him to give me his leg, but he pulled it close, tucking his knee under him. *Come on,* I said, *you can't leave it like that.* Leaning towards him, I realised I was lot taller than him. It's possible I seemed intimidating. He was shrinking back into the sofa cushions. I grabbed his leg under him around the ankle. I pulled it out. He looked away from me. I could feel his muscles tense up. I yanked his leg hard to straighten it. I got a good view of the scab; bright red and too new to be picked. He should have known it wouldn't come away easily. I took the loose edge and with one swift movement ripped it off.

He screamed. I knew he would. *Wait,* I told him, going back into the pantry where I knew I would find the first-aid kit – organised people are nothing if not predictable. I grabbed his ankle again, taking out the antiseptic cream with one hand, unscrewing the cap between my teeth and squeezing it onto the exposed pink wound. He yelled. I had hoped he would.

I smiled at him. *It's OK,* I said. *Here, let me rub it in.* I sat down next to him, rubbing his leg gently until all the cream was gone.

ANNA

What happened after I closed the gate, that was a mistake. Or a stroke of genius. Difficult to know the difference between the two sometimes.

My hands were shaking over how bad it had been to see her. Every time I saw her, it was worse. If Leo knew how often she came back, he would say I was losing my grip on reality. That was a phrase he was particularly attached to. Afterwards, he kept using it with everyone who would listen. He'd only recently stopped saying it; I wasn't going to tell him and risk him starting again.

I drove towards the junction where the farm track joined the main road. Approaching the junction, I saw a number of news vans with harsh white lights at the side of them, satellite dishes on their roofs, all of them facing out to sea. I stopped the car. Just to see what was happening. I couldn't work out what they hoped to capture – The Wave wasn't coming, it was just something for The Villagers to get excited about. Silly fears for them to indulge in. *The news moves in cycles,* I said to Leo, as if I knew. There had been waves all up the French coast the year before; huge things swallowing coastline, small towns; alert systems failing to sound in time. Devastating, they called them. We just wanted in on the action. A type of indulgent fear of missing out. This one, they said, would be bigger than any of them, the wave to end all waves, as if miraculously the sea would disappear. That's the way it goes with journalists, always looking for the next thing to obsess over. Soon, they'd be back to migrants, although we hadn't had so many of them, not since The Waves, which of course made it harder for them to come in their boats. Everything had its upside, I heard them say in the village.

When I got out of the car, I must have made a strange silhouette. Someone came up to me with a microphone in their hand, film camera over their shoulder. They looked encumbered, whereas I did not. I smiled at this deception. They thought I was welcoming them. They smiled back; *Are you from the village?* By then I was from the village as much as I was not from the village, it didn't matter I hadn't been born and bred there, plus, I really was an ideal candidate to talk on their behalf. *Yes, from the mill on The Spit,* I said. I wasn't sure if they were male or female. Short hair. Overalls. Hard to tell. *Excellent,* they said, *can I ask you a few questions? We're putting together a special feature about living in the shadow of The Wave.* It was then I noticed the initials on the side of the trucks, thought of the exposure. They'd need my name, my occupation. It would come up along the bottom of the screen, in capitals probably. I could ask them to make sure it was all in capitals, for emphasis. The reach would be immense, the exposure invaluable. I nodded. *Sure,* I said, *ask me anything, I'm more than happy to help,* which was how, in the days leading up to The Wave, I became a bit of a local expert – national celebrity, some even said later.

When I got back, the house was quiet. I tiptoed into the snug where Ava was sitting, Adam's head on her chest. He was sleeping, the way he used to sleep on Ada. I felt sick.

They both looked so peaceful, so settled. *Is it OK if . . .* I said, waving my phone at Ava, making it obvious I wanted to take a photo. *Sure,* she said, sitting up a little and beginning to smile. *Don't smile,* I said. *Just be natural.* Still feeling sick,

I swallowed. *Maybe just look down.* When she did what I suggested, they looked perfect.

After she left, I let Adam continue to sleep on the sofa. I sat next to him, putting a blanket over both of us. I looked at her on my phone, but I wanted to see a larger version. I flicked back to photos of Ada. She was not the right size either. Neither of them were animated; it was the movement I needed, to see either of them, alive.

I put the security footage on the big screen. Just to check everything was fine. I watched Ava in the kitchen, folding the laundry. She moved almost perfectly. I watched as she held one of my dresses against her. She swayed from side to side. Was she dancing? I watched as she looked around the room as if she was checking she was alone. I watched as she pulled her T-shirt up over her head, slipping my dress down in its place. Her shorts made the dress lie badly; she knew this. I leant forward; she bent down, pulling the dress up enough to get to the button on her shorts, then wriggled out of them. The dress looked better then. She moved around the room on her toes, making clumsy ballet moves. She was now all wrong, but also exceptionally sweet.

I had no idea who she was trying to be: Ava, Ada or me.

I must have fallen asleep, because when I woke later, there was Ada dancing in the kitchen on the screen, just playing over and over, some glitch in the mechanism. I sat up sharply, then realised how wrong I was; it was just Ava fooling around.

AVA

Walking home, I felt the outline of the scab where I'd put it in my pocket, cupping my hand around it to keep it safe.

As soon as I was in the front door, I checked the Value Meter. We were down to low double figures. I tapped it hoping that would do something. Nothing happened. I couldn't work out why our numbers were so bad. We hardly ever slipped into double figures. In the sitting room Mum was sleeping in her chair, her mouth open, some drool seeping out the side of it down on her grey top. She didn't wake up.

I took a fresh zip-lock bag from a drawer in the kitchen. I trapped wires from various, probably defunct phone chargers in the drawer when I tried to shut it; normally that would bother me and I'd mutter something about Mum needing to learn to wrap them around the charger heads before she stuffed them into the drawer, or how she needed to let things go, but I was in a hurry. In my room I wrote ADAM on the bag using a thick black marker, added the date too. I put the scab inside. I carefully ran the bag shut along the top with my nail and put it in my drawer with the other things I'd collected from other people, where I knew it would be safe.

In my room, I felt panicky about the numbers, and about how I was beginning to feel about Anna. Both those things, combined with how different her life was to mine, made me need something to distract myself for a while. I rolled up my right sleeve, felt round to the back of the top of my arm where a scab of my own was forming. I felt its rough edges under my fingers as I carefully began to pull it away from the skin. It wasn't ready. I bit the edges of the inside of my bottom lip as I kept pulling. Was this how it was for Adam? Is this how much I hurt him? I thought of Anna and the dog. How she'd kept going for too long. What made her do that? I wanted to know but I didn't like asking people things. They might tell me something I didn't want to know. Just because I didn't ask didn't mean I wasn't still thinking about it, trying to work it out. There was no reason I could think of for kicking a dog. I'd never hurt anyone apart from myself before. I didn't like how it felt and was struggling to think how Anna could have done that to the dog.

Finally, the scab came away. I put it in its own bag, dated it. When it came to writing a name on the bag, I didn't know what to put. I could write Ava, Ada, Anna. I just wrote, MINE.

I thought about Anna's antiseptic cream and how I'd helped Adam with it. We didn't have any, although I wanted some to numb the pain. I took one of Anna's pills as I began to scratch. I'd just cut my nails, which made scratching more noticeable. If you want a really effective scratch, you need something quite blunt, otherwise you just end up with a cut. I scratched as deeply as I could, over and over again. An excavation of sorts. On I went. And on. And on. I stopped thinking, the methodical scratching enough to occupy me. I scratched until there was no Adam, no Anna, none of my clients, nothing I needed to do for Mum, no Value Meter, just the scratching, repeating. It didn't even hurt. I stopped when I could feel my blood under my nails. I brought my hand round, surveying it by holding my fingers close to the lamp at the side of my bed. I would have liked to have pushed the blood and the dirt out onto one of Adam's slides, looked at it up close under his microscope. Things have a knack of being more beautiful close up. That's what I liked best about my client's faces, seeing them in parts rather than the whole. No one ever stays ugly if you see them like that. It's only when faces are far away that they become commonplace.

I put the bags in the drawer at the side of my bed, then reached under my bed and pulled my old treasure tin from under it. I used to store special things in it; now it was just my earnings. I counted it all carefully. There was more than I thought. For the last couple of years, it had just seemed like a vague idea. An insurance policy almost. I never thought I'd need to use the money, but it seemed like maybe it was time to start making a more solid plan.

It became clear to me that I was more like Anna than I wanted to be. Her with the pills to stop her feeling, and me with the scratching to stop myself thinking. It was reassuring to feel the itch as my skin knitted itself together a few days later, a reminder of how weak I'd been. As the scab became a bridge from one side of the scratch to the other, its predictability made the world feel safer. The dependability of the outcome, the certainty of it, became a kind of truth, and if it was a truth, there had to be other truths I hadn't discovered yet. All I needed to do was keep the faith that there was more to the world than this. It had worked with Anna. For so long, I'd never met anyone like me, and there she was, at the other end of The Spit, numbing herself, never content. It didn't matter anymore that she wasn't who I expected her to be or who she was through The Screen; she was something else altogether; she was exactly what I was hungry for. For years, I'd not wanted to eat anything – my body had shrunk and shrunk as I'd said no and no and no to everything – and now, I saw how hungry I was for so many things. I wanted it all, and the feeling of wanting was the most awful thing

I'd known. That evening, a thing I'd put to sleep and not asked to wake was burning in my chest. I wanted the world; it was the last thing I was ever likely to get.

I took another pill as I began watching her on my phone with the volume off – it didn't matter what she was saying; I just wanted to see her mouth move and the shape it made as she did so.

TUESDAY

WE

There was no air in the classroom that day; the heat made the other children restless and bored but the boy was fascinated by it; life, for him, was a thing of endless interest, a long series of puzzles he spent his time trying to solve; he was certain the sun had absorbed all the air, creating a new substance, foreign and possibly dangerous; he was convinced they were experiencing the beginning of the Heat Death of the Universe, a phenomenon detailed in a book belonging to the mummy; he didn't understand it fully as such, but something about the idea of entropy appealed to him, in part strengthened by the unmistakable fact that his mother was given to it; he knew already that things you loved died, and the thought of the world veering towards an inevitable point of collapse pleased him; there was a certain logic to this, and logic appealed to him; that day, with the windows open but no air moving past them, the teacher explained the various factors contributing to the unseasonable warmth; ozone layer, overfishing, beef, Paris Climate Agreement, fast fashion, industrial revolution, she droned, becoming background noise to these children who'd heard it all before; there was little point to hearing a thing when they couldn't do anything to change it, and so they played with the edges of their seats, rolled paper into balls before flicking it across the room; only the boy listened with his heart racing; something soon would happen; something strange and inexplicable was coming; he felt himself grow warmer, too warm; he would like to have unzipped himself from his skin, in the way he used to think was possible when he was a child, believing that somewhere in the surface of his skin a zip was situated and it would be simple to discard it, if only for a while, in much the same way a snake would slip easily from its outgrown skin; as a young child he had spent days searching for this zip, feeling down his back, convinced a mechanism was running down the length of his spine; he'd demanded the mummy unzip him because he could not reach round; laughing, she had patiently explained there was no zip, but belief did not come naturally to him; already thinking like a scientist, he needed proof; next he became increasingly sure a zip was hidden under his hair, taking the bumps on his scalp as proof, and so it was that one day he took all his hair off as the mummy slept downstairs, shaving his scalp badly with the daddy's razor, then running down to where the mummy slept, only for her to startle when a small boy covered in blood and tears woke her; there's no zip, there's no zip, there's no zip, the boy cried near inconsolably, his nascent faith impossible, the mummy struggling to come back from her gone-away world, staring at the strange boy, unsure if she should laugh or worry, telling him that, no, there is no zip, I told you there wasn't one – but still, tell a person something isn't real and it becomes the only thing they want to believe in; all that long afternoon he wished for the zip just as he was sitting wishing to be home because it was a Tuesday and Tuesdays were the day the mummy left him; he liked being left alone to his own devices, so much that his skin began to tingle with anticipation; he didn't care that at break time the children laughed at him, calling him soft as though he was a toy; they would mimic his voice and call out to him as they imitated it; nothing mattered on a Tuesday, and especially that one, with the anticipation of both The Wave and being alone compounding his excitement; as the afternoon stretched ahead of him, the boy was sure something was wrong with time, passing more slowly than it ever had, as if anticipating a thing only made it further away; he *tried to concentrate on the task at hand but the numbers on the board seemed to jump around; something wrong with time, with the weather, with his eyes; something wrong too, later, with his mother as she smiled and leered at him, but that hadn't happened, not yet, that was still hours away, but We felt it, We sensed it in the same way We knew everything on The Spit was wrong.*

ANNA

It became unbearably hot. I thought we knew heat, having spent so many summers in the city when the air would find itself pinned between buildings. But this was different. It felt like a wall, a physical object nothing could dislodge or move past. Adam kept calling it the Heat Death of the Universe. Leo said I shouldn't leave my books lying around; impressionable, he called him; fiction, I called it, but Leo was becoming increasingly convinced books were dangerous things. *Should come with a trigger warning,* he said.

I tried to tell Adam he shouldn't go around talking like that, but it didn't work. It was his most recent *obsessment*, as he liked to call them. Once he got a hold of something, there was nothing any of us could do to dislodge it. The only way was *through* with him.

I tried to reassure him it was just summer, and this was what summers were going to be like from now on. I told him we were so lucky to live near the beach. I gave him the facts, thinking they'd help – he had a head full of near-pointless information already; he could add these to his encyclopaedic mind. I said the recent heat increase was well within normal parameters and very clever people were working very hard to find a solution, but that wasn't enough for Adam. He refused to trust anyone other than himself. Leo said he was stuck at the egocentric stage. He suggested I might be too, and then laughed; I didn't. All Adam said was that he didn't trust the sea. With the news reports and The Watchers arriving in droves, this was understandable, but really, it felt a tiny bit restrictive, like it often did with Adam. He was suffocating. Like the heat.

I collected him from school and my heart leapt when I did because he ran at me. I wanted to swing him around, but he'd grown. All these things they do without you noticing, and so quickly too. I was in a festive mood, like I often find I am on Tuesdays. They make me giddy. It's hard to explain exactly why. I took him home, settled him down. I was so happy in that white-hot way you can be when everything feels like it's collecting in your chest and it might explode at any moment. I smiled at Adam; he asked me what was wrong. I laughed. *Nothing, silly,* I said, *Mummy's just happy.* He widened his eyes; I tucked him in on the sofa and told him he'd be fine; inside, things were popping and exploding the way they tend to do before the gaps come.

Before I left, I reminded Adam that, whatever happened, he was to phone only me. Daddy wasn't to know about this, the same as Daddy wasn't allowed to know about all the times he spent on his own in the house. The night before, with Ava, that had been good cover; Leo had said that morning it was good for Adam to learn to be left with other people. I'd nodded; Adam had kept staring into his cereal bowl. I couldn't have her coming every time I needed to go out – she was a sharp girl; she'd soon get suspicious. Adam was used to it; we had our routine, and it worked for both of us. So long as he didn't let anything slip, we'd be fine.

WE

After the mummy left him, the boy sat on his hands counting to sixty, seventy, eighty, just to make sure; every week, the same routine; telling himself he was going to resist temptation before always succumbing to it; his head began to spin the way it always did; he wanted to run, to be sick, to fall over; the excitement, having nowhere else to go, went straight to his head; full of adrenaline, he jumped to his feet, ran up the stairs to the mummy's room – a room she'd left in an uncustomary state of disarray, dresses strewn over the floor, lipsticks with lids missing, a trail of summer dresses, knickers, bra, as if she'd walked towards the dressing room as she undressed; the boy followed this gingerbread trail over the floor into the dressing room where the mummy's dresses hung according to hue, a rainbow of silk, wool, cotton; permitted fibres all of them still, although not for long; not for her polyester, Tencel, elastane; to the left of the hanging rail, rows of shoes with points so dangerous they could inflict harm if the wearer was so inclined; the boy ran his fingers lightly over the dresses, selecting one, two pairs of shoes, taking them into the bedroom, slipping out of his school uniform and pulling the dress over his head, breathing in as the cool silk settled around him, his feet too small to fill the shoes but not caring; he teetered over to the mirror where he became a parody of someone else; this is the way he learnt to slip from his skin, zip or not; he was freed of boy, became something other, something truer to his form, something lighter; he was performing no longer as the world became light again, so safe he could swear he heard his sister in the next room; a room that didn't belong to this house but instead to the one before; he heard her laugh; he closed his eyes, felt her ruffle his hair, was sure the warm den she'd made for him at the side of her bed was still there; he would climb into it later, rest on the cushions she'd stacked so carefully, wrap blankets around his bony shoulders; you're a good boy, she'd say to him, I'll keep you safe, and he'd close his eyes and sleep and all would be well; he knew it was possible to stay in that room for as long as he kept his eyes shut but he made the mistake of opening his eyes then and in the mirror was the mummy, leering, moving towards him, her face so contorted that she became a different mummy, a distorted one with wild eyes, with more teeth than anyone should have, with teeth bared and on show, snarling, spitting at him, mother turned to something wilder, shouting faggot, pulling at the silk, tearing the dress from the boy even as he shouted no; even as he shielded his face she did not stop until the dress was torn and ripped from the child's body, a body falling backwards through time and space, into the mirror behind that swung away from him, causing him to stumble to the floor; she grabbed the remains of the dress, strode out of the room as the boy sat with his chest heaving, the sound of his sobs ripping the heavy air.

AVA

It was sweet to begin with, to watch him. Once I got to know him, I nearly felt bad about it, knowing it could be construed as strange.

In the days after the dog, I'd watch when Anna brought him back from school. I wanted to make sure Anna was OK. She had such a brittleness to her, I worried she'd snap. And mid-afternoon's often a bit of a lull time for me.

Up close, he's so like Ada was, but with harder edges, a wider jaw, the same round eyes in a narrow face, the same sun-blond hair. Anna hardly ever posted pictures of him; it had always been about Ada, until she died, and Anna flexed, as she called it, to make it about the house, the sea, how living on the edge of nowhere had saved her – that kind of insulting crap. For people here, it wasn't nowhere; it was home, and the only one we'd ever get. I still liked to zoom in on photos of Ada, just to see the details, to check how well we matched.

When I watched them to begin with, I used to think there was something wrong with Adam. Anna was always telling him to hurry up or to pick his feet up or to get into the car, but after being with him, I realised he was just a normal kid. Maybe Anna expected too much of him. Maybe instead there was something wrong with her.

I was trying to get cool in the woods, but it was too warm even there. I was wearing cut-off shorts and a crop top. I didn't care about splinters as I climbed the trees. Any in my skin would be a bonus; I'd have more to add to my collection.

Up high it was even warmer. I watched Anna and Adam come home; hardly ten minutes later and Anna was out again. She was always going somewhere, barely arriving anywhere before she left again, as if it was impossible for her stay in one place for any length of time.

I couldn't see Adam through any of the windows at the back of the house. She'd obviously left him in the kitchen or the snug, certainly not in the sitting room they hardly used. I trained the binoculars on Anna's bedroom window, a simple large pane at the back of the house, the size of the loft door that used to be there.

She'd hardly been gone five minutes when I saw him moving around in the bedroom. It was difficult to see from up there exactly what he was doing. Not that I wanted to, not really, it was just too hot to do anything else. I felt languid, like I was trapped in honey.

His figure disappeared, then reappeared. He seemed to be getting undressed. I waited to see him in the outline of the frosted en-suite glass, thinking he was going to have a shower, but he quickly returned to the bedroom. He raised his arms as if in prayer and, slipping something over his head, shook himself. I saw the fluted shape of a dress settle over his body. It couldn't be anything other than one of Anna's.

I couldn't believe it; I needed to keep watching. He walked away from the window so I couldn't see what he did next. I leant back, looking out to the sea where it was as smooth as plate glass. More and more Watchers had arrived during the week. It felt so strange to think they were waiting for a single seismic wave, long anticipated, now scientifically predicted. Some of my clients had left the village at the insistence of their wives, but mostly, no one had travel exceptions left.

Nobody seemed to care, not really. It felt unreal in the same way the heat had until it arrived. We'd been living with so many little waves for so long that one slightly larger one didn't feel like that much of a big deal to most people. We watched disasters happening on the TV but couldn't connect them to ourselves. We were used to everything feeling far away, unable to understand how things affected us. Whatever happened elsewhere, life here carried on in its own predictable way. The way they were talking on the news, it sounded like a fucking tsunami; we knew that wouldn't happen.

Anna was hilarious now she'd become a newly self-appointed expert on it. She'd been posting all day, telling people to share her essential updates, begging for new followers, no one willing or able to see through it. The best part was, I knew she didn't believe it was coming, but she was acting like it was inevitable, like she had insider information from the fucking Wave. Like it had told her exclusively when it was coming. Some people would do anything for views; practically sell their kids, claim to be from places they hardly knew. The thought of it being exploitative didn't even seem to cross her mind. I almost admired her for it, the bare-faced audacity was, in a way, breath-taking.

The Watchers were good for the village, the shop, the pub. And for me, once word got round.

I couldn't decide precisely what I thought about The Wave. It scared me a little, but not as much as the other things I was afraid of. Right then the Deportation Bus seemed like more of a pressing problem based on the way our Value Meter was running down. The Wave seemed like a fairy tale compared to that.

When he came back, I raised the binoculars I'd brought to watch the swifts with again. Some of them nest at the side of the mill, close to Anna's window. Looking through them, I saw he was in a different dress this time. The length of it, or the distance I was at, made his movements look almost fluid.

He looked tiny but also special as he stood in front of the mirror, turning this way and then that, playing with his reflection like he was a kitten. Then Anna was reflected back in the mirror, standing just behind where Adam was, and he didn't see her, not to begin with and not until it was too late. Anna moved in a way I hadn't seen her do; she leapt across the room. I watched as she ripped the dress off him, even though he had his arms up so there was no need for her to be rough. She pulled so violently he fell back into the mirror in just his pants and those ridiculous shoes he'd put on with the dress. Then she was gone. Adam stood with his arms crossed in front of his chest. He stood like that for a long time before going over to the chair where he'd folded his clothes. His movements became the familiar jerky ones I was used to until he was a boy or a marionette, putting his clothes slowly back on.

ANNA

I went out and remembered I'd left my purse in my other handbag. I couldn't last another night without any – I needed my cards to get some cash. I sent a message saying I'd be late. I ran into the house and Adam wasn't in the snug where I'd left him. His stupid disaster movie was still playing on repeat. I shouted, *Adam*, but there was no reply. I looked in the kitchen; he wasn't there. I looked through the doors into the garden but couldn't see him there either. I went softly up the stairs, thinking maybe he was tired and had gone to sleep in our bed as he sometimes liked to.

Then I saw you, standing in the mirror the way you used to when you were little, decked out in my fancy frocks.

I opened my mouth, but no sound came out.

I stood, my eyes burning, as halos appeared around your head.

You floated away, again, not again, you were not going again, not so soon after you came back, I could not stand it.

You were only a mirage replaced by Adam standing, twirling, blowing kisses at himself in my dress. In my fucking dress, in the same fucking dress you used to play in, the same fucking shoes you used to totter around in, and I was over to him and then I stopped. I pushed the fleshy parts of my palms to my eyes. Remembered to calm my breathing. I said to Adam nicely and quietly, like the reasonable mother I was, maybe he could take the dress off seeing as it was one of Mummy's very special dresses. He refused to do what I asked no matter how calmly I asked him; perhaps I was a little more forceful than I wanted to be; when I try to remember, that part shows up as white, as if I've opened the camera door before winding the film fully back in; I can't be quite sure what happened, but what I do know is that afterwards, in the kitchen, I spread the dress out on the work surface, smoothed its fibres down, before I took shears meant for the garden, but it didn't matter, did it, what I used them for? Better to use them than not in a scarce economy. I took them to the silk; they moved easily through it like it was no longer silk but something soft – cream or butter. I cut every single piece of the dress up into smaller and smaller diminishing pieces, until it wasn't a dress anymore but simply scraps. I stuffed these new, unusable things into the bin.

Adam came into the kitchen, looking once more like the boy he was. I turned from the window where the sun was going down over the sea. Smiling at him, I asked him for a cuddle. He came over to me; I put my arms around him, but I couldn't make them soften. *Good boy,* I said to him, *you look lovely.* When I looked up, the sun appeared to be sinking into the sea. Sunrise, sunset, the phases of the moon, the moon's light – optical illusions, the lot of them. I still remember Adam's face when I told him the sky wasn't blue, just an illusion creating delusions. Poor child, you'd have thought I'd said Christmas wasn't coming. Sometimes, things just slip out.

What does it make you feel? I asked Adam as he stared out of the window, trying to make things normal. He looked for a long time, then he shrugged, wriggled free of my arms and took a knife from the magnetic rack by the stove. I watched as he sat at the island where he began to methodically carve into the marble surface. *It's late, you better get up to bed,* I told him. He didn't look up, just kept carving into the stone. *Stop,* I said, *you can't do that. Please, I'm sorry,* I added, hoping that would work, *about upstairs. I shouldn't have.*

OK, just don't do it again, or else, he said as he jumped up, brandishing the knife at me. I couldn't tell if he was being playful or not. He poured himself cornflakes, tipped milk all over them, then looked at them. *Actually,* he said, *I don't want these after all. Clear them up, woman, I'm going to bed.*

I tipped Adam's leftover, congealing cornflakes into the bin on top of the dress I'd cut up. I stood and watched the fibres grow fat and heavy and stained from the lactic acid, and maybe there were other colours of silk there too, reds and pinks and creams, but that might have been my eyes refusing to work properly, the way they kept doing all of those long, strange, heat-filled days.

AVA

I watched him leave the room. I should have been shocked to see Anna do that to him. But I wasn't, because after you've seen someone kick a dying dog, you know they're capable of anything. There was this detached quality to Anna; she was physically present, but little more than that most of the time. I wanted to know how she did it. The pills helped, but there was something more than that.

I saw her go into the garden. I thought I should check if she was OK. What I'd just watched happen looked intense. I was only checking up on her; that's all that was meant to happen.

ANNA

The worst thing about Adam wasn't that he was still here, it was the things he said. All this Heat Death stuff, he didn't even seem to realise how traumatic it could be for people. He was genuinely excited about the end of the world, in the same way The Watchers were enthusiastic about impending disaster.

Sometimes, I would let myself wonder if he was mine. When he was born, bloodied and blue, half spluttering, he was so perfect. Then they took him from me, wiped him off and cleared his lungs and did whatever else it is they do to the babies who don't breathe. When they brought him back, how was I to be sure he was mine? The baby they returned to me had the wrong nose. Ada's nose turned up at the end, and so did his when he was the blue baby, but the baby they returned to me had the wrong nose. I became fixated on his nose as the difference grew more pronounced the older he got, becoming a pointed triangle. Ada's nose didn't have a point, or mine, or Leo's; where had it come from, both the nose and the baby? I wanted to know. I'd stare at it in the long nights as he fed and fed and fed – he was an insatiable baby; I was never able to satisfy him. I'd wonder who he was, where he came from, how I could send him back and get my proper baby home.

And then it happened: my baby was taken, but not the right one.

Adam said he was big enough to put himself to bed and I nodded, so he took himself away; I took a bottle from the fridge.

No need for a glass. The sound of him crying, maybe, came to me from up the stairs. It could have been the foxes. A nightingale even; Leo had often said he heard them cry in the evenings. Likely that. I could barely breathe; I opened the doors to the garden. The hot scent of it – the flamboyant honeysuckle, the night-scented stocks, the sweet william and the lilacs – hit me all at once. It was too much with that and the heat. The lavender was the strongest smell, though. Always the lavender. Everywhere, all the time. There was no way to escape the weight of this place.

I took the bottle into the garden, went over to where the dog had lain and touched the lavender, its buds velvet under my fingers; it was tougher than it looked. I could see the print of the animal still there on the grass. Touching the lavender intensified the smell. I could have been sick.

The sight of its print reminded me of the toxicology report we were still waiting on for the dog. Poison, the vet had said to Leo when he'd telephoned, and they had to run more tests for the insurance. *Surely no one would want to poison the dog,* Leo had said, and I'd nodded, trying not to think how things had been missing from my bag, and the fucking dog had always been nosing around in there every time I left it on a chair.

Hey, someone shouted, and there was Ada, right at the fence. No, there was Ava at the fence, in cut-off shorts and a cropped top. It really was deliriously warm. I smiled at her, then looked away, so it seemed as if I was out there enjoying the sunset. *Pretty, isn't it?* Ava said, nodding her head over to the sea, and I made myself smile so she wouldn't know how much I hated the view. *Yeah,* I said, *really special,* but my head did something wrong; it shook itself from left to right.

Well, I said, and then Ava looked at me with her big eyes and I thought of Adam in his dress, such a flawed imitation. Ava was nearly the right height. The wine helped make her look almost perfect. I wanted to reach my hand out to where she was, just over the fence, so close, so temptingly close; surely there was a reason she was there; surely someone so perfect couldn't just arrive. I rubbed my eyes to stop myself rubbing her arm.

Everything was moving, just a fraction, as if there was a mole under the ground or something unsettling coming towards us; there was a distinct tremor. I said, *Do you feel it?* She frowned. I said, *I mean, the heat, it's so hot. God,* she said, *it really is; at least that should help,* and she pointed to my bottle and I laughed and took a swig so she knew I was still young, although there was nothing left in it. I noticed how brown her eyes were, such deep wells, things I would struggle to get myself out of if I stared into them for too long. It was these eyes that set her apart from Ada; Ada's eyes had been as green as mine, and Ava's were wrong in comparison to Ada's, but also, in that moment, absolutely right. Just a little while, just an evening, just an hour, just a drink, just this once; none of it would matter for as long as no one knew; I could wake in the night the same as I did all the time and make it unhappen. I smiled at her without any problem this time. I said, *Do you want to come in for a drink? You're old enough, aren't you?*

She laughed and said, *Yeah, mostly.*

I laughed back. She went round to the side gate, opened it and there she was, back in my garden.

AVA and ANNA

We followed each other into the house where we found another bottle. We drank it as we made holes of each other and into each other. One of us got another; there might have been one after that, but it was hard to keep count with the heat and everything sliding and slipping and coming undone the way it was when there was no longer anyone to perform for; shut up together just the two of us like we were, it felt more like a holy communion than anything else, with the blood of Christ washing us clean. Something like that.

We crossed more lines then, so many lines, and there were packs of pills chased down with his bottle of whisky that burned our throats and we stroked each other's skin; that's all we did; it was too warm for anything else.

AVA

That Anna, she's fucking mental. And I thought I'd met all sorts.

ANNA

The dry-mouthed dawn came for me the next morning. I woke and, stretching out on the sofa, discovered a hole where Ava had been. Or where she might have been. The last thing I remembered was the garden, the bottle, the gate and the shit sunset; the rest, only spaces where my hunger controlled.

I ran my fingers over my bare legs where I could still feel her skin. I licked all the way up my arms, but they tasted only of sweat and not of inside things.

I wanted freeze-frames this time. I wanted stills. It's always the things I want back that are the things I lose. The things I want to hold onto become the gaps. Sometimes I think it might be a good idea to get hypnotised. Just to help with my memories. Leo says, *Best not.*

I shut my eyes; nothing, not even flashes.

Perhaps I went to sleep. The sound of the curtains rattling against their pole startled me and Leo was standing at the window, backlit black against the white morning light. I put my hand up to shield my eyes; *Is there any need?* I said; *Wow,* he said, *that's how it's going to be.* Adam trotted through clutching his lunch bag like it had his life in it. *Mummy doesn't feel too well, does she?* Leo said to Adam while staring directly at me, his eyes a recrimination.

I tried to stand up, but my legs wouldn't comply; they buckled and sat me back down on the sofa. I giggled, drew the corner of my lips together, my top lip folding over onto the bottom one. *Well,* I said, *I seem to have a little bit of a problem getting up.*

Leo shook his head. He was wearing a new suit. He looked good. All his running was paying off. He had his ID round his neck. I started to laugh, thinking of the old saying about doctors' children dying. It was so not funny it was nearly very funny. Fuck. *You look just like God,* I said to him, *standing there all illuminated like that. I'm taking Adam to school,* he said, then he said something like, *I wish you'd not let him see you like this.* He talks in clichés. *OK, Lord,* I said, saluting before falling back giggling on the cushions, exceptionally pleased with my joke, but he didn't laugh.

He sat down next to me, began flicking through the channels until he reached the CCTV. Even the light coming from it was too bright. *What are you doing?* I asked him, sitting up sharply. I couldn't remember if I'd turned the downstairs camera off last night. I knew upstairs was fine; I'd sorted that weeks ago. *I'm looking for last Wednesday,* he said, *to see if I can figure out what happened to Pongo. You're quite the detective,* I said, trying to make it into a joke, but he was skipping through the days, back to that morning, until Pongo was there grainy on the screen but still unmistakably taking something from my bag, nosing it over the floor. *Leo,* I said, but he didn't look at me. He just kept staring at the screen as Pongo tried to rip the bag with his teeth and, suddenly getting a taste of what was inside, eagerly ate the whole thing.

I realised it was imperative to look innocent but not so much so that it would look forced or fake. I was also trying hard not to shake from last night and from the shock of knowing exactly what had happened to the dog. It's one thing to think a thing, another to know it. I stopped playing with the edges of the blanket. It seemed to make the most sense to stare right at Leo when he looked at me. He wouldn't expect that. I didn't blink as I looked at him. *Anna,* he said, *it looks like Pongo found something suspicious in your bag.*

Leo –

It looks as though you have a lot you need to sort out, he said quietly to me, leaning in close. It was worse that he was quiet. He used to shout. He didn't now he claimed to have tamed his anger; if I raised my voice, he'd say, *Anna, anger issues*, tilting his head to one side and widening one eye. *I'm going to get Adam his breakfast,* he said, *and you're going to get dressed, and we will erase this recording and hope the toxicology report remains inconclusive, otherwise someone is in a lot of trouble.*

I tried to stand, but still my legs were useless. I was still slouched there when Adam came through with Leo behind carrying Adam's lunch box and school bag. *Give your mummy a kiss*, he said; *Mummy, you smell funny,* Adam said; *Doesn't she just,* Leo said; I pretended not to hear, then Leo leant over like he was going to kiss me, but all he did was whisper in my ear so Adam wouldn't hear, but he misjudged his volume as he snarled, *Sort yourself out by the time I get home, otherwise, this time, I really am done.*

I rolled back on the sofa, pulled the blanket up around me. *Yes, captain,* I said, before closing my eyes.

I think he shouted back into the room that he'd be home later than usual since it was Wednesday and he was working late, but I was already feeling down the back of the sofa for my back-up pack.

AVA

The mistake I made that evening was to need to touch her. I have this problem: if I like what something looks like, I need to touch it; it wasn't any different with her. As I reached my arm out to put it on hers in the garden, I could see the caterpillars moving under the webs. I wondered if Adam had ever shown them to her.

Her bruises really put me off. I know I pick my scabs just like everyone does, but it was extreme to have so many bruises. Even so, it seemed like a good idea to try to keep something of hers to store when I got home. That's why I scratched her so badly, to get some of her under my nails. Her skin was still there later when I ran a cotton bud under them the way I'd seen them do on police procedurals. There wasn't much to look at, but it was enough to know her cells and DNA were there. I put it in another zip-lock bag; it felt good to write her name on it, even though I knew by then she was mad. I liked souvenirs; didn't mind where they came from.

Afterwards, I didn't want her anymore. It happens sometimes – you think you want something, then realise you're wrong. The following day, I sat in The Way Tree, flicking through who she followed on The Screen. I thought of Mum buying towels to copy people she saw on it; was it possible Anna's life was an attempt to look like someone else's?

Anna was too popular to follow too many people. That was the rule: the more followers you had, the fewer people you followed. Me, I didn't follow anyone; that way no one could follow me. I didn't have a profile picture either; there's safety in anonymity.

Clicking on other profiles, it didn't take long before I saw that they all had nearly identical houses. Unnerving, Mum would have called it, like she did the heat, the migrants; this time, she wouldn't have been wrong. I wanted to know who they were all copying. Someone had to be leading them.

ANNA

When I woke the second time, my silk top was stuck to my back. I stretched my hand round and felt how wet it was. I could smell last night sweating its way out of my body. The white-hot light bouncing from the crystals Adam had hung at the window for luck split into cold, sliced-up rainbows dancing over the walls; they made my eyes pulse. I shut them. I lay, half asleep, remembering Ava lightly stroking my bruises before she kissed them.

Then I began to see things that hadn't happened. I opened my eyes. Sat up.

I was a new-born giraffe when I stood to go to the toilet. I sat on the lid and peed all over the floor; it stank of wine and whisky. I was too tired to clean it up properly. I just kind of rolled a towel around the floor in the hope it would soak it all up.

A shower seemed like the best idea. I let it run before I stepped in. I wanted breath-stealing cold. I opened all the windows but there was no air to come in. I checked the Carbon Meter but there was none left to spend. *Fuck!* I shouted as I banged my hands against the wall. I used to complain about fans, about air con, but I'd kill my fucking dog for some, and then I remembered about the dog. I had basically killed it. I didn't do much to help the poor fucker, and my track record was a bit chequered after Perdita, which maybe explained Leo's preoccupation with the insurance, but, fuck, dogs were difficult. I slid down the wall to the floor. Even the floor was burning – no wonder they have those ugly marble tiles in Italy; God, if it gets worse here, we'll have them next, fuck, fuck, fuck, imagine the actual horror. I started to laugh, thinking of dogs and the way they needed walking, all the fucking time. Man's best friend, like fuck; like, I'm the one who had to make it look like I'd walked the fuckers every single day, and two of them at that. Children, at least, were easier. So much harder to kill.

Fuck.

Not exactly.

Fuck. I needed to start paying attention. Real shit was happening too in the world. Leo kept going on about it, even Adam was better informed than me, but God, the internet was beguiling; it was easier to post pictures of the linen closet and the renovation, and I was practically a fucking national hero for the work I'd project managed on the mill. And now, I was the latest pundit on The Wave. It was easy to be impressive online, where people never needed to meet you or see how much you really knew or didn't about real life. People on The Screen were finally beginning to take me very seriously. I discovered it didn't really matter what you said or how much you knew about a thing; so long as you sounded like you had a certain amount of gravitas, people lapped it up. My accent was an advantage, always had been. News editors had begun to follow me; next stop, maybe I could wangle a book deal. I'd look good at a launch. Could talk about how painful it had been to share my story, but so very worth it even to help one other person.

Leo said it wasn't a real job, not like blood on your hands. He loved that line, like he was more valiant than most because every day he *did* have blood on his gloves. Not like he wasn't being paid a fucking fortune for it, securing all our futures. And yes, I was grateful for him, like he needed me to be, but God, he didn't need to trot out at every opportunity how much better than everyone his job made him.

I tried telling him there was an art to the photos I took. People thought it was easy, that all I had to do was snap something and put it on The Screen, whereas in reality it was difficult to construct a whole other version of reality. Probably easier to cut people open and stitch them up again; at least you didn't need to try to stay ahead of the competition. He didn't seem convinced when I said that. He laughed at me, as though I entertained him.

I objected to his accusation that I didn't tell the truth on The Screen. He liked to say it wasn't real, or that I manipulated reality, as though life outside of The Screen was only a series of verifiable facts. I wanted to scream at him, to pull at my hair, to tell him that his new love of nature was nothing other than a distortion; the countryside wrapped up like it was all green, everywhere, all the time, full of swifts arriving home, fresh water to swim in; everything living in perfect harmony and unity. What they left out was the ugly side of it, everything vying with each other trying to survive, how there was no inherent morality to nature, just one long game of survival, the fittest always fighting their way to the top. And if he thought here was better for people, he was only fooling himself. He'd been led astray by all the nature books he'd stocked up on, all of them neglecting to mention endemic intergenerational poverty, lack of opportunity or entrenched racism. No, it was the sea, the tides, the pull of the moon; no real-life problems, distortions of reality; they'd always been everywhere. We all survive by buying into a long series of lies.

The sin of omission – everyone was at it.

Same with having children – no one tells you how that'll be.

If they did, who'd do it? There are all the practical books about looking after babies that may as well be fairy tales because the babies haven't read the books knowing how they're meant to behave: to feed every four hours and nap the rest of the time. Or the mad hippy nonsense about tying your baby to you like it's some kind of ornament to carry around all the time; how damaged it'll be if you ever leave it to so much as whimper. Those books should be burnt. Someone should write one about the strange desires you get after the baby comes, the way you think about sinking your teeth into its neck, inflicting a quick fatal wound like a cat might, or the urge that comes to fling it down the stairs, to hold it under the water just a second too long until the bubbles stop rising to the surface. The incessant pull and push of being a parent, the division between caring for them and the inevitable way it obliterates who you were. How the boredom and the bone tiredness eat into every part of you, how it drives you insane so quietly you don't see it creeping up until it's too late. The first time we went out after Adam was born, I realised I was sitting in the middle of a bar rocking gently; I was so used to getting him to sleep. Tiny madnesses – this is what loving something so intensely does. Did.

Then it happened. I'd wished for a life without them but there's a reason they say be careful what you wish for, because she was there and then she began to fade as if disappearing before my eyes. I did not know how to stop her erasing herself; she was obliterating herself and making me watch; she was torturing me for all the things I couldn't do, her protracted effacement becoming a taunt, highlighting all my failings. They talk about people being snatched away from you, but Ada wasn't; she took herself away, denying me my single beautiful daughter, atrophying into something uglier, death writing itself on her face as her skull showed beneath her skin, until it was all I could see; I could not fix her. The air of expectation hung over the house for months; we knew it was going to happen, we just didn't know when. It was enough to drive a sane woman mad.

Weak, I sat down in the shower, the water soaking me, the skylight open, impotent.

It soaked my hair, dripped into my open mouth. I tried to remember to tell Adam about that later. When the spring rain was really bad, he'd asked how it was you couldn't catch rain on your tongue, but you could snow, then he'd gone around with his mouth open all the time trying to catch the rain. I told him it was something about the temperature of your mouth and the snow and the difference between the two being what you noticed, but he didn't want to listen. Adam knows best. I started to laugh thinking of the strange little fucker.

I was all goosebumps when I stood up; I turned the dial up as high as I could and for two minutes I watched the water drip down my shoulders, between my breasts and over the stubborn dome of my stomach, down to my feet, and I could've stood there watching it forever after the light joined it and made it almost beautiful, but the carbon alarm set in with its insistent wailing and the heat cut out.

Blinded by the water in my eyes, I pulled a towel off the rail, dried myself, went through to our room, or my room now Leo calls the spare room his den, *Like Daniel*, I said, getting biblical, but he just looked at me strangely.

There were shoes and dresses all over the floor and bed, half-pushed-up sticks of lipstick on the dressing table, and it was all a bit strange, as if I'd left it in a hurry. Either I couldn't remember what had happened, or I didn't want to think about it; instead, I lay down with my hair soaking through into the pillow and stayed there, with the sheet half on, half off, half too hot, half deathly cold, and closed my eyes as all the gaps from last night began to piece themselves together, like the mercury we used to keep in a jar when I was little, and I'd shake it and watch it part, then coalesce back into a tight ball, over and over, and Mummy would pick me up and time is a thing to fall through and into, so long as you know the trick.

FRIDAY

ANNA

After I dropped Adam at school, the hours blurred, like Fridays can.

After, but before it was time to get Adam, I went to do the weekly shop. I don't know what was wrong with me; all I know is everything seemed far away and inconsequential. The air had a new quality; in thickening itself as the heat grew it had changed weight, becoming too heavy to swallow.

I sat in the car, trying to remember why I was there. I wanted to be elsewhere. Nowhere specific, ten years before maybe. I put the music on, tilted my chair back, took a drink from my water bottle, set a timer for ten minutes on my phone. When it rang, I was still there; in some way Ava was too. I couldn't make her go away. My head was heavy and sore and hot; it felt like a thing I couldn't hold up anymore. I was so full of Ava, so sick and full there was nothing else I could see when I closed my eyes, there was no food I could swallow past her; it was all her and only her; my fingers smelt of her and yet didn't smell enough of her. I wanted all of her and none of her. I wanted to eat her up; I wanted to spit her out.

The sun spilled into the car; I pushed my palms hard against my eyes to keep it out; I saw a spectrum of red, white and yellow, with pink dots pulsing against the changing background colours. I could have sat like that forever; maybe I did sit there for a long time – I don't know; time was luminous in those other-worldly between days as the heat grew and grew and grew and something in me did too; some forgotten thing stretched and yawned and showed its teeth, its claws, its hunger.

The music finished. I took my palms from my eyes, slid the smooth pills from the pack and rolled them between my fingers. Something was happening to the ends of my fingers. They weren't working. When I touched things, I couldn't feel them properly, as if the outlines of them were blurred and indistinct, as though my fingers weren't sensing properly. I put the pills between my teeth to check their solidity, but even then they were not firm and certain as they once had been. I crunched down on them and tasted nothing. I chewed and chewed and chewed more and more feverishly, but still nothing. Sweat beaded itself on my brow. I swallowed.

I opened the car door and left the vehicle.

I saw my reflection in the other cars parked there, but even that seemed to be a thing elusive and uncertain, there one moment before it slipped and swam away from me. It seemed impossible that the distorted reflection in the steel, catching and shining with the high sun, originated from me. This uncertainty had an obliterating effect, throwing my solidity into question in much the same way as when my mother had taken me to the fairground when I was three or four or five, surely not six; if I'd been six I'd have been old enough to realise it was a trick, just a contortion of the glass, but I wasn't old enough; instead, the illusions I saw led to an abiding fear of my reflection. I stood in the House of Mirrors, watching as my reflection grew longer and thinner in one mirror, wider and fatter in another, waved and disjointed in the next. After that, distrust crept into everything. If I couldn't trust the basics of my reflection, then what else wasn't real? When I looked in the mirror I began to imagine I was fatter, wider, uglier than I was. It became second nature to see things that weren't there, distorting my own image with the strength of my imagination. I didn't think I could have just looked away. No one asked me to stare at myself. I walked over to a car where my squat reflection strode towards me, looking around itself as it did; observing that the car park was empty, I raised my foot, began to kick the car. Myself and my reflection kicked each other, the metal buckling. I walked swiftly away as the alarm caught on the air.

As soon as the cold air in the supermarket hit me, my arms became pimpled with goosebumps. I rubbed and rubbed them, but the air conditioning was too strong; there was nothing I could do to warm myself up. All this regurgitated, repeated air turned me to ice.

I walked around the home electric aisle, picking things up, thinking I could use this thing or that thing, although all the words on the packages seemed to make less and less sense, the uses of the things becoming more and more uncertain; a black box begged me in neon writing to *take the future home*, but I didn't understand what was in it. I put it back on the shelf. When we bought Adam his phone the box had written on it in gold lettering, *Elevate reality*. I kept walking.

Things became even more confusing in the fruit aisle. South African apples nestled crisp in their plastic packets; a shaved coconut sculpted into a cup complete with a straw – paper of course; fruit from places I couldn't locate piling up on the shelves. I remembered we were eating local and seasonal, but all I could find were potatoes; the onions were French, the lettuce Dutch, the strawberries Spanish. Before we arrived, we said when we did we'd order a box from a local farm, but after we moved we found all the agriculture had gone. Leo couldn't remember reading about the decline of British farming; *Couldn't have been a fashionable cause,* he said, raising an eyebrow at me. He was always talking about me and my onscreen friends, how we jumped on causes for a full five minutes before moving on to the next one. *Regular little white saviour, aren't you?* he said when I put Activist in my bio for a while, which I thought was unfair since Black lives did matter.

Having no better option, I had to stick with the supermarket and what they offered. Leo said I needed to be careful with the Value Meter; the wrong food registered on the Carbon Meter would make our numbers go down, but it wasn't like we didn't have enough to play with. He was becoming obsessive with it, the way everything tipped into obsession with him, checking it all the time for fluctuations, getting alerts sent to his phone.

I thought I could get some beef. Make steak and a potato salad. Something easy. Leo hardly ate meat, especially red, although he said we needed the vitamins every once in a while, *Especially you, Anna,* he'd say, passing the buck to me, making the purchase of something so unethical my fault, when I knew how much he loved the taste of raw meat. That was one thing he thought was worth eating into our carbon quota for.

The meat was lined up in refrigerated rows, freeze-wrapped in plastic, pink and gelatinous. I looked around to check no one was watching; the other women were pushing their trolleys up and down, down and up. One had a baby half hanging out of it; the mother looked dead-eyed, knackered. I nearly smiled at her. She walked past me, her head down, eyes to the floor following the unspoken rules of forced proximity. Once they were gone, I thought I'd check the meat for freshness. I poked it hard. Then harder. The cellophane wrapping stretched under the force of my finger as it sank into it. The resistance of the cellophane made it feel as though the meat still had tendons, muscles. It was strange to think this flesh had once been a living thing, changed now in form but not function, born only for this, to end up imprisoned on a supermarket shelf. I'd never thought about it before, until there I was, poking a dead animal.

I did it to the steak; I did it to the cubed beef; I did it to the mince. The more I did it, the less it seemed possible it was a dead thing, just as it seemed impossible it had ever been a living thing either. It was simply something for dinner. Something to feed on, something to fill me up. I picked up a packet. Sniffed it. It didn't even smell. I'd given birth twice, I knew what blood smelt like; every month I was reminded of those hollow rooms, the rubber floors, the screams coming from the woman next door while I would not, did not, do not, scream. How was I meant to know this was meat if I couldn't smell blood? I could not trust it.

I wanted to see blood, fat, sinew. I wanted evidence. I wanted organs. Bone, carcass, skin. Leather, hide, suede. Maybe the butcher's counter would be better. I pushed the trolley over to it, battling with its wheels, which insisted on going in the other direction, my teeth chattering from cold and excitement, my hands shaking slightly. I couldn't remember the last time I'd eaten – yesterday maybe, but what? I wasn't sure – a peach maybe, or a pear; a plum perhaps; something along the lines of the book I used to read to Ada.

The butcher's counter didn't help. There was no blood there either. I remembered the sharp metallic taste of raw meat and the effort needed to chew it into smaller and smaller pieces before it slipped down my throat; I wanted that, but not this. When the butcher asked if he could help, I asked if the meat was prepared here. *Yes,* he said, *just through there,* indicating to the plastic sheeted doors. *Can I see?* I asked. He took a step backwards away from me. *No,* he said, *you can't.* I stood trying to think of some way of asking him where they put all the blood; did they have a use for it, or did they just pour it down the drain for it to clot itself up? But he was busying himself with knives, sharpening them over and over, and I knew that meant I wasn't to ask him anything more. I can be too much sometimes, for some people.

Leo said under no circumstances were we to eat fish; something about microplastics, mercury, ethics. *Who do the oceans belong to after all?* he said. *Impossible to demarcate the fluid.* I nodded like I agreed. I like fish. I like prawns. I like peeling their skeletons away. I like how they wear their bones on the outside. I thought I'd buy some, or some langoustines, although I'd reacted badly to them last time and the room had spun; I think it was them, at least.

The fish stared up at me from the ice, their eyes clouded, their scales grey, silver and blue. They didn't look dead; they didn't look alive either, or as if they ever had been. I stared and stared at them. The woman behind the fish counter came towards me, her hair trussed in a stretched net, covered by a white peaked cap, wearing white overalls as though she should've been on a surgical ward and not here. *Can I help you?* she asked; *One minute,* I said, and then I picked up a fish, a small salmon or a large trout; it was heavier than it looked, more solid too; I liked the feel of it. I squeezed it hard. I didn't look up but I could feel her watching me. I knew what she'd look like when I did meet her eye; her face would wear her disgust. Its flesh didn't move much, not like the beef, its buried bones holding it in place. I looked up. I was right: the woman stood stock still staring at me, her upper lip slightly curling. I smiled at her as I held the fish to my nose, inhaling deeply. *So strange, don't you think,* I said, *that you can't smell the sea on them?*

Madam, she said, *unless you plan to purchase the fish, I suggest you put it down.* I thought of throwing it at her, of the bruises it would leave, but it seemed a shame to spoil such a beautiful fish. Its skin really was a thing to behold up close, so I put it down. I was bored of the supermarket and its strangeness, and the strangest thing seemed to be that I'd never noticed or known how odd it was before. I turned around, knowing she was still watching me as I walked away.

Even the silence seemed to have its own particular sound and weight as it pressed on me. I was on my way to the drinks aisle when I saw you.

There you were, pushing a trolley along just six feet ahead of me. If I hadn't stayed so long at the fish counter, I would have missed you.

I hung back for a moment, ensuring it was you. I had been getting it wrong so often recently. But it was unmistakably you. I knew I wasn't wrong. It could only be you from the way you shifted your weight from side to side as you walked. I pushed the trolley as quickly as I could towards you, but the wheels still refused to cooperate. You were walking faster than I was; if I didn't hurry, I'd miss you. I abandoned the trolley and ran up to you, throwing my arms around your shoulders, and you turned around to me, alarmed, and I smiled, about to tell you it was OK, but it wasn't OK because it wasn't you.

Oh, my baby, my fucking baby, always appearing and disappearing.

I apologised hastily; the girl walked briskly away towards her mother.

I went back for the trolley, walked to the drinks aisle and stood looking at the brightly coloured bottles, knowing none of them could deliver what I needed them to. I was beyond their reach again. You were working as an echo; I didn't know where I ended and you began. I never had. The night you were born I'd watched your tiny movements, entranced by the way you stretched. The way you'd moved when I'd been pregnant made so much sense when I saw you. I felt as if I'd known you for a long time. You were always so familiar, in a way your brother never was. Your little hands the same as mine had been when I was small, your eyes and smile too; all these familiar parts moving around in a body outside mine. It was always too unsafe. I knew I couldn't look after you. Not really. There wasn't enough of me. You grew; I couldn't keep up. And now, where were you? It was impossible that someone so fierce and full of life could be gone. I couldn't bring myself to say what you were; for as long as I didn't say it, it couldn't be true. You would come home soon, I knew it. I had your room waiting for you with your clothes and shoes ready. I kept myself small enough to try them on sometimes, just to check we still looked the same. I needed you to come home soon; we would go shopping for new clothes. Make a proper day of it, as we always had done. I hadn't cried for you because what they said about you wasn't true; I would not cry for someone who was only waiting to come home and you would you would you would you would you would you had to you would soon soon soon. I pushed the trolley as hard as I could into the bottles and walked away as the sound of glass reverberated around the great hollowed space, followed by shrieks. I walked out of the supermarket, grabbing a bag of pear drops near the door. Someone shouted at me. I didn't turn around. I walked back to the car, switched it on; *Hello, Anna*, it said, *are you ready to free your control?* before driving me away.

WE

The mother didn't talk about it after it happened; this is what she did, for as long as a thing remained unvoiced, it couldn't be real; the boy, though, wasn't wired that way; for him, a thing unsaid grew in size, blocking out all other thoughts; that's why all he could think about after the sister disappeared into his mother's silence was his sister; she filled his dreams and his waking hours to such an extent that some days he was sure she had returned to him or he was back with her, unsure as to what house he was in when he woke, as if time was a permeable thing he could easily slip through; the mother was excited, distracted, speeded up when she collected him from school, some days, she flapped her hands around, her green eyes more piercing than they had been recently; this transformation scared the boy; he knew it foreshadowed nothing good; her dress was carelessly unbuttoned at the top, purple bruises on show; he stared at them, worried the mother had hurt herself, easily forgiving other hurts as children too readily do; hastily she buttoned herself up; he knew something was about to happen, something unpredictable and likely terrible, although he wasn't sure what as his mother told him to get into the car, smiling brightly, telling him they were going on a big adventure, an awfully big adventure, the BEACH, she exclaimed, as if this was a treat, the boy beginning to reel off his list of reasons he hated the beach: too hot, too cold, too warm, too sandy, too unpredictable, too many people; the mother, feeling under the passenger seat, panic rising as she couldn't find the parcel, leaning further and further down until she couldn't see out of the windscreen, the boy asking what she was looking for; fuck, she shouted, one hand fiddling with buttons, the other reaching under the seat as the car said, Anna, welcome to the ride of your life; the boy leaned forward, picked up the paper bag that had slipped into the back of the car, asking, is this what you're looking for, the mother grabbing it from him, driving him towards the sea.

ANNA

As the car drove itself, I needed something to distract me, so I checked The Screen. I'd picked up a few thousand followers since I'd spoken to the press about The Wave and it looked like I'd managed to convince everyone I was a local expert. That morning, I'd posted photos of The Watchers, showing how they were arriving in droves. Some of my diehard followers had commented that they were on their way; *See you soon,* they exclaimed. Everyone desperate to get in on the action. I didn't tell them how disappointed they'd be when they got here.

I remembered after we lost Ada how well people had responded to it. Everyone loves grief. I became an expert in it, even changed my bio to Grief Expert for a while. Ran a few courses about recovery and resilience. They sold really well. Everyone loved Ada; she became a viral sensation for a while after. I scrolled back to photos of her. She really had been so photogenic.

I hadn't shared any photographs of Adam in such a long time. I couldn't stand to make my grid about him when it had been about her for so long. But as I scrolled, I realised I was missing an opportunity. There'd been a flurry of criticism over people sharing photos of younger children – consent; detractors liked to heckle – so I played along, scoring more points for not displaying Adam than I would've for posting him. It was important in my game to keep up, to stay current, keep my content relevant. I remembered how he'd looked the other night in my dress, the way he could almost have been her, and everyone loved gender-fluid kids; he'd practically handed me a gift.

I told the car to go faster. Before I collected him from school, I stopped at home. I ran into the house, stuffing what I needed into a bag, filling a hamper full of crisps, juice and fruit, grabbing my big camera.

He was meant to be excited. The beach was supposed to be a treat. He should have been grateful to do something special after school. But he hates crowds, and it was full of people that day. Rows of them sitting on chairs on the sand all the way down to the tide line as if the sea was a cinema screen. I took him down to where the sand was damp and packed hard, the ready-made audience facing him. He should have been excited when I pulled the dress out of the bag and held it up to him. But he just wrapped his arms around his chest saying he didn't want to get changed with so many people watching. When he finally slipped the dress on, The Watchers on the beach broke into applause, most of them holding their phones up to take photos of the moment. He refused to pose for them or me; instead, he became a startled animal. *Run to the sea,* I told him, and as he did the dress billowed out behind him; I ran alongside, snapping furiously, hoping to catch the movement of the silk, his puffed-out chest. I knew they'd make beautiful images; I wasn't wrong.

Back at the car, I told him to take the dress off. He wriggled awkwardly out of it in the backseat as I posted photos of him with the caption: *didn't think he'd be wearing my clothes so soon,* knowing people would love it. In the rear-view mirror I watched him caress the silk; I told him of course that was just for fun, he wasn't to wear my clothes again, and he nodded, making his eyes wider, which seemed to be his latest trick. I wasn't sure if he was trying to make himself look innocent or like an innocent victim. Either way, I wouldn't be tricked by him.

WE

They made a strange sight when they arrived at the beach, the mother striding ahead of the boy struggling under the weight of a picnic hamper, a tripod, a large striped bag, the mother unencumbered in linen dress and straw hat, smiling at every stranger she saw; as with all strange sights they quickly gathered the attention of the crowds lining the beach on chairs facing out to sea, waiting for The Wave; how we laughed at them, The Watchers, eagerly awaiting their destruction; the attention intensified when the boy and the mother passed the signs saying Expected Tidal Zone, walking down to where the sand was packed hard from the last tide, the mother saying this is where we'll shoot, the boy hating all her shoots – perfect for capturing precious memories, she liked to say to him, as if there was some deficit with her memory, as if she needed photographs to recall anything at all, the boy and the daddy often excluded from any of her memories, only space for her and the sister on The Screen; the boy thought her a fool for this, knowing there was no way to escape from memories, knowing he had little power over them either; there was no way for him to determine the things he would hold onto versus the things he was certain to forget, the pleasantness of the recollection having little to do with his ability to assimilate it; in fact, the opposite was often true; it was the least pleasant things he often found himself recalling: the day of the ants, playing over and over; the mother's leering face; long afternoons alone – he needed to find a way to make them stop; the mother shouted as the sea made the perfect frame behind them, put your bags down, take your shoes off; the sand warm and wet between his toes; perfect, the mother exclaimed as she set up the camera, checking the light meter, pulling the dress from the bag; as she held it up the boy thought he would be sick – so close in style to the dress she'd pulled from him – hardly able to believe it when she told him to put it on, hesitating to take it from her until she said, put it on; she commanded again and the boy, unsure then of what to do, took off his T-shirt, slipped the dress over his shoulders, suddenly self-conscious, with The Watchers assembled as an audience; from under the dress he took his shorts off; some of The Watchers stood to applaud, others to take photographs of the touching scene they would later upload to The Screen, only for them to go viral days later, the boy's face a lasting emblem of life on The Spit, some filming the mother as she instructed him to DANCE; the boy's movements fluid then as he danced for the crowd, forgetting himself for a moment, inhabiting his body in the way only silk would allow him to, his feet fleet and fast across the grains of sand ground so long ago; the strange boy from the mill, lost and found there with the sea behind him, blue and still; nothing foreboding about it that Friday afternoon, unfolding as any around there might, but that's how secrets were kept there on The Spit, in full view, so as never to be seen apart from by eyes like Ours, eyes that knew how to see beneath and beyond.

AVA

I felt shaky when I left my Friday 4 p.m. He liked to meet at his house, which I didn't usually permit. The first time he'd asked, I'd said no, but he said he'd give me double for indoor work – it was a tempting proposal. I cut him a deal, said I'd need to give him a test run outside, just to check I could trust him. Outside, he was all sweetness and light, and I thought about the money he was willing to give me, which was pretty substantial. Double would really affect my profit rating.

I was so close to my savings target that the risk felt worth taking.

I'm not sure that it was. There were things involved that I hadn't expected. Chains, whips, studs. They hurt.

I was almost used to it, but that Friday I was tired. It'd been a heavy and confusing week, with Anna and curved balls, and I'd been so thankful for my Wednesday 7.30 when he'd texted saying, **Can we do the same as last week?** and I'd replied, **Sure, yes!**

We sat in the tree and watched the sunset and as we did he told me facts about birds. He was shocked when I told him I didn't know all of their names. I told him I knew robins from Christmas cards and woodpeckers too, not that they'd survived, and he told me about swallows and swifts and how to tell the difference and the way they all had their own distinct calls and showed me this app on his phone that played all the different songs and how it's the males that sing, not the females, which felt kind of like the wrong way round. He said, *That's why the male birds are always so beautiful and sing so well, to attract the females.*

That explains why the females are always kind of dull and quiet because they have to blend in on account of predators. That's kind of what happens, isn't it? I said, thinking of Mum. He went quiet for a while, then nodded and said, *You might be right.*

I told him when you've lived in the countryside all your life it's hard to romanticise nature, it's just *there*. But also that learning their names made me feel kind of strange, like I was separating them into groups, and I didn't feel good about doing that. It felt like such a human thing to do, a way of creating a hierarchy. *Like Adam,* I said. *What about Adam?* he said really quickly, like he was falling over his tongue. *Naming the animals and shit while Eve stayed at home,* I said. *Oh yeah*, he said, *doesn't seem quite fair.* After we'd said everything there was to say, we watched the sun set the same as last time, but this time it felt a little bit sad. Last time, it felt like a world opening up with so many things we could say, whereas this time we were in The Way Tree, neither of us knowing what to say next.

Still, seeing him was the best part of the week. Everything else felt unstable, like it did when I'd first been on a ferry over to France and when I got off the boat the land felt like water, and it took days for it to feel firm again. That's how I felt when I wasn't with my Wednesday 7.30. I looked forward to being with him, which was a bad sign.

All of that goes some way to explaining how I felt when I left Friday 4 p.m.'s house and took my water bottle from my bag and opened the lid and swirled the water round and round to try to get rid of the taste of pee, which was one of the drawbacks of being paid double.

I took my phone from my pocket to quickly check what Anna was up to. There Adam was on The Screen, even though she never posted pictures of him. Standing and looking right into the lens, with 2,583 likes already, was Adam dancing in her dress at the beach. Underneath the photo, the caption: *didn't think he'd be stealing my clothes so soon.* It didn't make sense, but then I was beyond expecting Anna to hold to any sort of logic.

The pavement stuck to my feet as the tar was melting, the smell making me want to retch. He looked so like Ada. I was careful not to hit the heart button. I switched profiles and went to her stories, where she'd posted all the outtakes with lots of cute GIFs, and then there was a more serious story from in her kitchen, posted only ten minutes earlier, where she was leaning on the marble surface, her head on her hand with the light perfectly bouncing off her cheekbones and a glass of wine at her side, the glass covered in condensation. She leant forward, speaking in a hushed voice to let all her followers know she'd had a big talk with Adam, who'd realised he wanted to start building his digital presence, but in a controlled way. It was his narrative to own, she repeated, especially pleased with that part. I was too distracted by the way her lips moved to hear the rest, but, fuck, he looked so like Ada.

Just like Ada. So much like Ada that he nearly looked like me. It was just our eyes that were wrong, I hated how brown mine were. Had she realised how like his sister he looked? Was that why she did what she did to him the night she caught him in his room? Did she mistake him for Ava? Was she angry at him for it? I'd thought it was because of what he was wearing; I thought the sight of him in a dress was enough to make her incandescent. I hit my chest to try to make myself breathe. My breath felt trapped. If he looked like Ada, she could dress him up; she would take all her love out on him; there would be none left for me. There would be no need for me. Soon, one of us would edge the other out; I didn't know who. I just knew there wasn't space for both of us.

What need would Anna have for me if she could make Adam be Ada and not me? There would be no Ava then. I was not ready to give this up.

I went home to wash. As soon as I opened the door, I could tell the leak under the sink was getting worse. I could smell the damp and wanted to think that was what was affecting our numbers so badly, but I knew there was something else. I walked through into the kitchen and Mum was there, under the sink, with everything from the cupboard around her. She pulled her head out when she saw me. I frowned. *Shouldn't you be at work?* I said. She sat up, wiped her hands on her top. It was wet under her armpits and in the middle of her chest. *I'll put the kettle on, shall I?* she said. I shook my head. *Is all right,* I said, the same as I said every time everything was terrible, *I'm off out.*

I knew then she'd lost her job again, and that's what was wrong with the numbers. I didn't want to know what she'd done this time. It hardly mattered anymore. There weren't any jobs she could do that paid enough for our Value to ever be any good. We only ever scraped by with our numbers. *You don't exactly help,* Mum liked to say, even though the doctor still said I was too ill to work and I got Value Credit. I told myself it would be a relief to have the Deportation over and done with. I'd spent so long worrying about it happening, I just wanted that feeling of lightness that comes when something's finally done. I didn't want Mum to be gone, but at the same time, it felt like I'd spent most of my life trying to look after her and she was pretty resistant to being looked after; it didn't matter how hard I tried to help her, she always fucked it up. Maybe that's how I learnt to look after myself so well.

I ran out of the village, along the length of The Spit to the mill at the end, slowing down as I arrived so it would look like I was just out for a walk. I sauntered past the kitchen window; before I reached the end of the house she was out into the garden with her arm in the air, waving to me like she had when I first saw her. Only this time she wasn't doing it like she was made from paper; this time her arm was free and fluid. She shouted my name and I went round to the side gate thinking it would be weird for a moment to see her again after her madness the last time, but when she touched my skin all my hairs stood up; I knew everything between us would be just the way it was and just the way she wanted it to be; her affection for Adam was all for show; nothing could make up for the real thing; Anna needed me and always would. I was safe with her; all I had to do was keep her wanting me. I needed to stay indispensable.

AVA and ANNA

In the house, we dressed Adam up. We took him upstairs and began to play with him. He was always so desperate for attention, but when we gave it to him he didn't even have the good grace to look like he was having a good time.

His mouth was smiling but his eyes weren't. He seemed heavier than a boy his age should. When we put the music on and told him to dance his movements were all wrong. It became almost painful to watch but that wasn't enough to stop us. We kept saying, What about this one? How about that one? *changing the song, insisting he dance to faster and faster rhythms as, growing tired, he danced more and more slowly.* Adam, *we shouted,* look, look, *as we held diamonds up to him, clipped earrings to his ears, draped his neck with scarves.*

He didn't say a word. He just looked at us and when we told him to look in the mirror, he looked at the floor. One of us shouted Adam *again as the other one hit him just hard enough to make him look up and he stared in the mirror at us, his eyes telling us to stop but we were too far gone by then. There's a point when something happens and you can't go back, not without saying to the other* we'd better stop this *because to say that would be to infer that the thing you're suggesting you stop is wrong, so neither of us said it, not wanting to admit that this next thing we were complicit in was worse than the first; instead, we continued as it became unclear which one of us found the wig or which one of us put it on Adam's head; who suggested the lipstick is also not clear, or the mascara or the eyeliner or the eyeshadow, but the end result is easy to remember: Adam standing, weeping, ruining the overall effect.*

If he hadn't cried, he'd have looked just like her, then we could've pretended we were all in the room, at the same time; the impossible would have been made possible, the three of us all where we needed to be, Ava, Anna and Ada.

But he did cry. He did ruin it. He stood there, weeping, weeping, weeping. One of us hit him to make him stop; which, it was impossible to tell. He didn't stop crying; they wouldn't stop hitting. One of us held the other's arms back to try to make them stop; flailing arms beat the air. Exhausted, Adam crumpled to the ground. One of us picked him up, carried him over to the bed, where he curled himself into the shape of the foetus he'd once been. We sponged the make-up off him gently. As he retreated into sleep, we lifted his floppy arms, sat him up to slip the dress over his head, then left him in the room that had become a litter of clothes, shoes, make-up and jewellery and one little boy, marooned in the middle of his parents' bed.

PART II

WILL AND PLEASURE

Nothing touches but, clutching, devours.
– Ted Hughes

3 | THE PARK

It masks the absence of a basic reality.
— Jean Baudrillard

AVA

Anna couldn't breathe after what she did upstairs. It was stressful for her to see Adam looking so much like his big sister. It wasn't normal. She brought wine from the fridge, poured us each a glass, put the bottle carefully in the recycling.

She sat too close to me, the smell of her sweat enveloping me. We were both sweating from the heat and intensity of upstairs. I wanted to cry. Everything was too heavy; everywhere was too hot. I couldn't let her see me like that. I drank the wine quickly, but it only made everything less distinct than it already was. *More?* she said. I nodded; *Please,* I said, holding out my glass, and she walked away into the kitchen, her thin viscose dress showing the shape of her legs as the light turned to honey.

I couldn't stay here with these insane people. It was only a matter of time before I went mad too. Or before I was deported with Mum. The Value Meter was a serious problem I kept returning to. When I heard the sounds of Anna moving in the kitchen, I suddenly knew what I had to do.

I've only ever been sure about one thing before. That was when I set up my business. Everything was going wrong with school, I'd lost my appetite, the doctors merged my Value with Mum's, then said until I was measurably better I could use hers. I made sure I wasn't measurably better, that way I could avoid getting a job anyone knew about; creating one for myself was the only way to have a reliable income.

I'd been so focused on money until Anna came along, and then I'd shifted my focus to her, and everything was going wrong. I couldn't let things slip. She was getting in the way. I thought about the woman she copied. I'd finally found the one they all looked up to, Olivia from New York, with 1.5 million followers. Every idea Anna had seemed copied from her. Right down to half the courses she ran. Olivia had lost a child as well and had developed several courses around grief. A community, she liked to call it. Olivia was also younger than Anna and, if the photos I'd saved were anything to go by, far prettier.

When Anna went into the kitchen it was as if she was vanishing already. I sat for a while, then I stood up and pulled my phone out of my pocket where His number was safe from the time I stole it from Mum's phone, where she kept hold of it so she could chase Him about maintenance every month. I checked to see when He'd last been active, like I did every day so I could monitor if His number changed or not. *Last active 25 minutes ago*, it said, and there was a picture of Him with his arm around some kid that I supposed must be my sister. Last week it had been a picture of a different kid. How many of them were there?

I put my phone under my leg, face down, so I wouldn't do what I wanted to do. I knew it was time; the urge had opened its mouth. I am no good with urges. They devour me. In the kitchen the fridge door clicked shut. I heard her rinsing glasses. I picked up my phone. I typed, **Hi, Dad, it's me**. I deleted it. She clinked the glasses together as she picked them up. I wrote, **Hey, Dad, it's Bethany**.

Closing my eyes, I pressed send, swallowed the bile in my throat and put my phone back in my pocket.

Anna came in, put the wine down and started with her

fingers on my knee. Wanting more of me. *We don't have long,* she said, *before he's back from work.* She told me he carved people up all day. *Glorified butcher,* she said. I tried to imagine him: he'd be middle-aged, beginning to put on weight, his belly hanging over jeans he'd say still fitted even though he did them up under his belly, using a belt to keep them up. He'd say things like he needed to get fit and he'd take up running from time to time, that's what he'd be like. Anna wouldn't care, though. She had the house and the clothes and the car and all the things his money could buy and now she had me too. Weird, I never thought of charging her. Maybe I could sort of bring it up in conversation, see what she said, talk to her about arrears. Shame I didn't have any photos of us together to prove what we'd been doing. If he didn't look like that, he'd be super-skinny with long arms and legs, but also blank-looking since Adam and Ada were all Anna. His genes wouldn't be that strong. He'd be nervous, do things like pick at his skin maybe; have a tic, for sure, something that grew out of years of being bullied at school. I'd seen too many doctors in the last two years to trust any of them. They were always so convinced they knew everything, certain everything could be fixed, seeing problems where there were none, refusing to see problems where they really were. Poor Anna. No wonder she was so fucking insane.

Distracted, I didn't realise she was touching me; I returned her kisses often enough for her to think I was paying attention. When she was finished with me, as she wound my hair around her fingers, she said, *I have an idea, why don't you stay the night? We're going on a trip tomorrow; it would be so much fun to have you there.*

Something ran down the length of my body. I didn't think it was a premonition, but it could have been. Certainly, I didn't feel

OK. I said, *Are you sure?* She told me of course she was and that I could sleep in the spare room. I said, *I'd love that, I'd love it so much,* I said, kissing her more enthusiastically than I wanted to. She showed me into the bedroom I'd seen the first time I went to the house. I didn't dare look at my phone. I was beginning to feel stupid for sounding too keen to Him. Like a stupid kid. I thought about slapping myself like I used to, but the bedroom distracted me.

The room was something else. When I sat on the bed the duvet was soft and thick beneath me. I could feel the feathers in it. I lay back, let it hold my body for a moment.

She closed the door softly behind me, telling me to wear anything I found that I liked in the drawers. It was then I saw the wooden name plaque on the back of the door: ADA, it said. She'd put me in Ada's room. She had a room for Ada. Was she waiting for her to come back? She really was criminally insane.

Still lying down, I took my phone out of my pocket and rested it on the inward curve of my stomach. I thought about turning it over. I thought about looking to see if He'd replied. It made me feel sick to think of Him looking at my messages, deciding if He wanted to reply or not. I shouldn't have sent it. I knew it was stupid to think He'd save me. Mum said He'd never wanted me. *You were meant to be a boy,* she liked to remind me. *If you had been,* she'd say, with her eyes all watery and her words slurring together, *then he'd still be here and I –* and she'd swing her arm out in a grand, sweeping way so I knew just how dramatic the situation was – *and I,* she'd repeat for extra effect, *wouldn't be in this mess now, would I?*

Then I'd hug her and pull her into me just like her mother should have and kiss the top of her head. I'd get toilet roll for her eyes and whisper that everything would be OK. I'd tell her I was there to look after her. She'd look up at me after a while and ask me to pour her another drink.

Fuck. I was betraying Mum by even thinking of Him. By having His number; by sending Him a message I couldn't take back; by not letting her be enough. *You always,* she said, *want so much from life; what is it about you that makes you think you're so special?* she'd say as she scraped my dinner into the bin.

On the bed were three pillows stacked on top of each other, immaculately aligned. I put the phone under the bottom one. I couldn't decide if the house was perfect or if it was too much. I wondered if it would have driven Ada mad. There's maybe only so much perfection it's possible to take until you want to scream. This was a house people didn't scream in. Not out loud, at least.

I made myself go to sleep. It was too hot and I'd had too much to drink for sleep to come easily. I kept surfacing; I needed some of Anna's pills. They always worked when I couldn't sleep. I woke, and heard Anna and her husband in the bedroom, banging the headboard against the wall. She sounded enthusiastic, like she liked what he was doing or what she was doing or what was being done to her or what she was doing to him. I put the pillow over my head to block them out.

When I heard them, it felt like something was beginning to undo itself inside me. Or outside me. I knew this sound meant she wouldn't keep me. I was just another thing to her. I hadn't been wrong when I'd thought that after she'd posted the photos of Adam. I needed to learn to trust my fucking instincts. It was safer to leave before she told me how bored she was of me. She didn't have it in her to want anything for long. Or not the things she had, at least. She was more attached to the idea of things than the things themselves, only really ever wanting what she didn't have. That's why Ada meant so much to her; she was something to cry over and want back.

That's why I pulled my phone out; why I hit the home button. His message was waiting for me. **BETHIE! My sweet girl. Are you coming? I saw the news. YOU MUST COME before The Wave gets you. HAHA. Your dad. xxx**

I put the phone down. I picked it up. I put it down. I picked it up. I put it down. I picked it up. I gripped it hard as the sweat on my palms made it slip. My heart hammered up my throat. My hands shook. My legs too. My whole body. He wasn't meant to reply.

I went to my messages; my brain was blank. I wanted to think of something clever to say. Something that would make Him laugh. Something that would make Him think I was smart. But all I wrote was, **Yes, I'd love to. I have money. I can pay. Xx**. I deleted the kisses. I wrote, **from Beth**. I deleted that too. I wrote **from Bethany**. That didn't work either. I tried **from your Bethie**. That looked better.

After I sent it, I put my phone back under my pillow and tried to swallow. I slipped one of Anna's pills from my pocket. I felt the cool metal of the bell from The Way Tree. It usually made me feel better; that night, it didn't.

I padded down the hall to the bathroom, every surface reflecting my face. My eyes looked bruised I was so tired. These were the things she did to me; how stupid I'd been to think of her as a good thing. I put the pill between my teeth, my mouth over the tap, the water a cold relief as I swallowed.

Back in the bedroom my fingerprints became things of new interest to me. It suddenly seemed so strange that I'd never cared or stopped to look at them before, these things that were probably the only part of me that was properly mine and yet

I hadn't ever paid attention to them. Was it a lie, about how unique they were? Like the myth about snowflakes, when they discovered they weren't all unique after all, just that there were so many hundreds of varieties it had appeared they were all different for quite some time. Something like that. I read so much that it's hard to remember it all. My brain isn't the same as it used to be either, not after last year. I don't hold onto things like I used to. Still, the likelihood of billions of people with different fingerprints seemed pretty far-fetched. Humans, they'll accept anything if you say it with a serious enough face.

After I got tired of thinking about my fingertips, I took my phone out again. He'd sent a message back. **NO NEED! Save your money for yourself. Ticket booked for SUNDAY. Travel exception all filled in. NO NEED TO DO ANYTHING. Love you so much. Dad.**

I tapped my fingers against my phone. There wasn't much to say to that.

Love you too. Did you tell Mum?

NO!!!!!

Do you want me to?

No. I'll tell her in the morning. How long for? xx

I'll buy you a return once you're here.

I'll be wearing my red Stetson

. . .

YOU WILL NOT BE ABLE TO MISS ME!

Haha

Bet you have missed me. I have missed you, little Bethie.

YAY! Can't wait.

When the online marker next to His name went, I started to scroll through Olivia's feed. She was the most original thing I'd seen on The Screen. Olivia was clearly much Higher Value than Anna, her New York Brownstone renovation project so much better than Anna's mill restoration. I felt a bit sorry for Anna, thinking of her being stuck here, but then I had to start thinking of myself again. Anna was history.

I fell asleep feeling detached from my body. That was the best thing about the pills. I woke and watched the swifts outside the window layering mud onto the nests they'd built there, repeating the same task over and over and not even minding.

ANNA

When he came home, I was on the sofa.

He leant over me, took the bottle from my hands and kissed me. I flickered my eyes open like I didn't already know he was there. He kissed me. I kept my mouth shut to keep the taste of Ava in. But I was tired. Slowly I opened my mouth. He took this as an invitation the same way he always did, pulling at my wrists, his hands tight around them, until I was standing and limp and somehow I was being dragged up the stairs to the bedroom, where I was on the bed with him on me, taking off the clothes I had left on; I think he might have used his teeth, as if he thought this made him more of an animal; he was looking up at me as he did, his eyes wide like he was trying to say something as he slid my silk pants down my legs. I just wanted him to hurry up. I was used up and done from earlier. It didn't take long before he was sweating and frictionless, but his sweat soon stopped and our skin started to slap slap suck as we stuck to each other; it was an organism of its own beyond our control; who was doing what to each other it was impossible to say. Did I invite him in? I don't think so, but then, in the mirror, at the blurred edges of my vision, there I was, arched feet and tensed legs, repeating over and over until I was the spider I'd watched only that morning, making its web, layer upon layer upon layer with its legs bent and deadly; I smiled at myself as I thought that. I wanted to be slick enough that I didn't feel any of it, I wanted to be outside my body, but I was on the comedown already; the timing was all off; all I could feel were the sensations returning to my legs and the effort he was making; I was too still and contrite. Something needed to be done to help it reach its logical conclusion. We might have made a noise; the headboard wasn't attached as well as maybe it should have been. He might have been saying things; I might have recited my part of the script. After all, we were well rehearsed. He gets all his best ideas from porn. At least he'd stopped telling me to sit on his face. When that was his favourite line I would be up there, holding onto the headboard; every time I looked down, he'd be staring up at me, just another thing to watch. It was off-putting. After a while, I kept my eyes straight ahead. That night, I was pinned down, the slapping sound growing in horror and momentum until all I could hear were the effects of his intensified labours, his skin on mine, his hairs curling and darkening with his sweat that had returned now he was working so hard. The more he burrowed into me, the more I realised his convex stomach filled my concave hollow. It didn't used to be like this; it wasn't meant to be like this. Suddenly he saw stars, sparks. The void opened its mouth, showed me the depth of the darkness, the sharpness of its teeth. This never happened with Ava. He grunted, rolled, was off me and was wiping his brow, biting his mouth with his wide-spaced, square tombstone teeth.

Wow, he said. I smiled at him and rubbed his arm for a minute, before turning on my side and closing my eyes. I heard him moving in the en-suite. I was safe. Sleep came, bringing strange dreams with it, dreams where everything was moving; I dreamt of faces I was sure I'd never seen, so many of them, leaning too close to me, leering. I woke, although I could still have been dreaming that he was beside me with his stomach nestled into my back, the outline of his penis at my buttocks. He had one arm tight over me as if hoping to hold me in place for the length of the night or longer; he muttered something that might have been *night, darling*, but I couldn't quite make it out; I tried to wriggle free but the weight of a sleeping arm really is too much.

SATURDAY

AVA

In the morning, I stretched, pulled on my shorts and tied my hair back into a ponytail, feeling my feet sink into the carpet. The way the other people live, never realising how much they have, and none of it ever enough, nearly made me laugh. I bit my lip to stop as I walked down the polished wooden stairs holding onto the banister. Anna had polished it with something that smelt of honey. I leant forward to smell it better, then I walked through the snug and into the kitchen, where my Wednesday 7.30 stood drinking coffee at the kitchen island.

Bethany, he said, looking at me, his coffee flying out of his mouth into the air, dropping to the floor, as Anna turned to stone at the open fridge door with the blue light on her face.

ANNA

Bethany, he said to Ava, like he too had mistaken her for someone else. *No,* she said, *I'm Ava.*

I closed the fridge and took orange juice over to them where their silence seemed to be contrived somehow. I watched him as he licked his lips. *Isn't it funny?* I said as I poured the juice into glasses. *She's the spit, isn't she? Of whom?* he said, which is how I knew he didn't see it; she just looked like any old teenager to him, just like some Bethany he'd patched up and forgotten the details of.

Did he even remember Ada? He didn't talk about her to me. He didn't talk to Adam about her either. Did he sit in the mess room at work and talk to his colleagues? I didn't think so. He'd just obliterated her like he did everything he didn't want to acknowledge.

An anomaly, he'd called her, resistant to treatment, he'd said, in the same way the other doctors did; undisclosed trauma, they'd said in family therapy when they'd tried to make me talk about myself and how I'd come to be the person I was. I'd bitten the inside of my lips to make sure nothing could get out; I was not going to be made a scapegoat of. It's always the mothers they come after, that's what I said in my course: How to Be Your Best Self with the Time You Have; it sold out in fifteen minutes, back when I was at my peak, before Ada happened.

He put his glass next to the dishwasher.

I said to Ava she can come with us, I said. *Yeah,* he said, *did you? Good,* and he looked at Ava, whose eyes were wider than they usually were. *That'll be fun,* he said, and she said, *Yeah, it will, Adam'll love it,* and Adam looked up from his cereal bowl, the skin around his eyes looking more purple than I was happy with. *We need to get your strong medicine in you,* I said to him and he nodded, moving his eyes between each of us as we spoke.

Can I have a quick shower? Ava asked. *Sure,* Leo said. *There are towels at the top of the stairs; the bathroom's at the end of the corridor. Thanks,* she said to him, running out of the room, never looking back at me.

I heard Leo in the pantry. He was checking the Meter, obsessed as he was with our numbers. *Anna,* he said, *come and see this.* I went through and he was just staring at the Meter. I looked. It said seventy-eight. *Doesn't make sense,* I said. *It's missing at least three digits. I know,* he said, *has to be something wrong with it. I'll call the Data Centre.*

When the house phone rang five minutes later, I thought it was the Data Centre calling back. I was in the dressing room deciding what to wear, so I didn't bother getting it. Then I heard him on the stairs, bellowing in a way he hadn't for months, ANNA, ANNA, WHERE THE FUCK ARE YOU, ANNA?

He stormed through the bedroom to where I was standing in my bra and pants. *Fucking hell, Anna,* he said, *that was the vet on the phone. You know Pongo ate enough coke to –*

Kill him? I said. Sometimes, you're in so much trouble, there's no point trying to swim back to shore. I just gave up then; I'd been drowning for years – it was about time I let myself sink.

It's all a big joke to you, isn't it? Anyone could have found that coke. Imagine if it was Adam we were talking about and not a dog. Do you know what that would do to our Value?

187

Oh, fuck you, I said, pulling a dress from a hanger. *Imagine what it would do to our VALUE. Is that it, is that what you care about? How it affects some fucking arbitrary data set? Good God, you're so fucking sanctimonious the whole time and that's all you can say?*

That's not what I was saying, and you know it. You have to twist it all, don't you? he said.

I don't know, I said. *When I say a thing, I like to make sure I say what I mean, that's the point.*

I'm not doing this, he said, walking out of the room the way he always walked out of the room. *But I'm not getting another dog. Fucking disastrous, expensive mistake that turned out to be.*

Cunt, I said under my breath. When he asked what I was mumbling, I said, *Nothing.*

AVA

In the bathroom I turned the shower on. It ran cold. I turned it up, thinking they were High Value, they could do what they wanted. Nothing happened, except I heard the Carbon Alarm ring down the corridor, then Anna ran to it, swearing. I bet she used up all the hot water.

I stood there in the freezing water, shivering until I got used to it. I wanted to make time go backwards. I wanted it to be before Anna and her constant location tagging, her continuous posting, my insatiable curiosity. I wanted the long nights of scrolling back through Anna's life to unhappen. I wanted to delete it; one swift click and it would go away. I pressed my forehead to the cold tiles, shut my eyes, but when I opened them I was still there; it was still real. Through clenched teeth I whispered, *fuck fuck fuck fuck fuck fuck fuck,* drawing each one out as I went.

It didn't help.

I was ruined. My Wednesday 7.30 was Leo. Anna's Leo. I'd taken to thinking of him as mine. I was beginning to value our conversations; the thought of him having a similar connection with Anna wasn't one I wanted to have. Did he sit in trees with her too? Did he caress her bruises? Did she touch him, when he wouldn't let me do the same to him anymore? She'd taken him from me. I was glad to be leaving them both. Just one more day and evening and I would be flying away from this place, away from the pathetic intricacies of their little lives, away from the way they hated each other, away from the boy they were screwing up, away from the heavy memories of the daughter they did the same to, away from The Watchers, from The Wave, from the sheer fear of the Value Meter. Away.

It was so warm I was wet again by the time I'd dried myself. I dried the sweat and guessed it didn't matter too much since I was wearing yesterday's clothes. There was no way I was wearing Ada's clothes like Anna clearly wanted me to; how had it taken me this long to realise how actually fucking psychotic she was?

I used Anna's or Leo's bamboo toothbrush and powdered-charcoal toothpaste. It was black when I spat it out. I rinsed the sink, catching sight of myself in the mirror; I smiled. Ava or Ada or Bethany or Anna smiled back. It occurred to me that if I had to spend one last day with them, then I may as well make it one to remember.

Everything was so fucked, it didn't matter what I did; nothing could make it any worse. In search of ways to make it better, I opened the vintage medicine cabinet with a bright painted red cross on it; Anna had probably spent weeks tracking it down. I knew Olivia would think it was tacky. She'd have something sleek in her bathroom. There was nothing exciting in the cabinet.

I rummaged through the woven baskets on the reclaimed scaffold-board shelf and there, tucked under towels, were the same pills I'd been taking. I thought of taking two, but it wasn't like I was going to see either of them again after that day; by the time Anna knew they were missing, I'd be gone. I slipped the whole blister pack into my pocket. Just in case.

In Ada's room, I looked at my bruised thighs; the left one had at least ten scabs on it, the right was more purple than anything else; it probably should have hurt. I began to pick the first scab, telling myself I could pick five of them, save the other half for later, but I got carried away; before I realised, I'd picked six scabs. There was blood under my nails; without thinking, I wiped it on the duvet cover, leaving tiny pink flecks behind.

My phone buzzed with another message from Dad.

I'll be the one in the WHITE Stetson.

Bought a new one today to mark the occasion.

xx

I was already beginning to feel like things that weren't funny were funny, so I sent Him one back with lots of laughing faces.

Then I put my phone next to the pills in my pocket and skipped down the stairs, smiling, to make the most of our last day.

ANNA

My head started to pound in the car. There were too many people. Ava and Adam in the back, me and Leo in the front. It would have been polite of Ava to leave after she heard us in the bedroom, but she wasn't one for picking up on social cues, that girl.

We had to stop for The Watchers. The road was blocked by their camper vans, caravans, lorries. More press had arrived too; they didn't care about traffic, they just wanted to get the first pictures of The Wave to stream around the world. It almost looked like it was coming after all. In many ways I felt relieved at the prospect.

Do you think we should stop? I said, checking my lipstick in the mirror. *I could give them a quick interview.*

For fuck's sake, can't you just let it go for a morning? Leo said. *We need to go, it's Permitted Mental Wellbeing. Essential, some might say.*

Fascism, Adam shouted from the backseat. I turned round to him. *Sorry,* I said, *what was that? Fascism,* he said. *A— Someone said once that the wellness industry is just covert fascism. Think about it, who decides what wellness is, and how it is enforced? It's just another narrative, isn't it?*

I closed my eyes. Wished he'd stop regurgitating every half-formed teenage thought Ada had ever had.

Leo was more patient. He was in a giddy mood that morning, as if something exciting wasn't just about to happen but *was* happening. *That's an interesting observation, Adam,* he said, as if it was Adam who'd observed it, *and yes, there are many ethical and moral drawbacks to the proliferation of the wellness industry, not least of all who's qualified to teach.* A dig at me, well done; I thought about applauding, then I remembered Ava in the backseat. Instead, I looked out of the window. *But there are certain things that are classed as pathologies,* Leo said, *and therefore are illnesses, and doctors, like myself, help people with that, which I think we can agree is a good thing.*

Fucking Leo, after a medal for doing his job again.

It's all very interesting, Leo, said Ava from the backseat. I looked at her in the wing mirror. Was she flicking her hair over her shoulders?

I felt under my chair for the bag, just to check it was still there. It was. I itched the bruises on the left of my chest. *You OK, Anna?* Leo said. I nodded. *Fine,* I said, *just my head's a bit fragile. Happens,* he said, looking at Ava in the rear-view mirror. He was – he surely wasn't? – winking at her. I ran my middle finger over the fading teeth marks. I always felt naked when they started to go; that's why I needed to replace them so often.

By that time the police had cleared The Watchers to the side of the road. I craned my neck to look back at them as we drove past. There were so many of them, all convinced they were going to see something spectacular, and soon. It was almost sweet, like an eleven-year-old on Christmas morning, desperate to still believe.

There are pills in the glove compartment, Leo said. *Oh, are there?* I said, convincingly surprised. *Thanks.*

I took two and then slid out another two without anyone noticing. Next to the pills were the pear drops I'd taken from the supermarket. I opened the bag, reached round to offer Ava one. She refused, Adam took one; before long the car smelt the way Ada's breath had. I opened the window. Ava kept smiling and chatting and playing with the ends of her hair, but it was OK because by then I was so far away I was watching her from another planet. Leo started talking about the clashes at the Sorting Centre between the activists and the protestors. *Horrible to think there are some people who believe we should send them home,* he said; from the backseat Ava nodded. *Them,* I said, but they didn't hear, or if they did, they didn't react.

When we arrived, the theme park shimmered in front of us as if it was movable, something I couldn't grasp. I was sweating by the time we were lined up politely in the priority line. I was sure my sweat smelt of wine and last night. In the park Adam scampered ahead of us. *Don't run on like that,* Leo shouted. *We don't want you to get lost.*

AVA

I'd been to the park once before, when I was little, with Dad, and maybe Mum, but it was a slippery memory, one I couldn't quite trust. More like a memory of a memory than anything close to fact. I smiled, thinking I could ask Him about it tomorrow, and Leo smiled, thinking I was smiling at him.

It was fucking surreal, that's what it was, to be there with them. The pair of them hating each other, and each hating me too, for the way the other was looking at me.

Poor Adam was skipping on ahead. I still liked him, even though he clearly was a sick little fuck. I kept finding maimed birds in the woods. I felt bad about what we'd done to him. I didn't want to feel like that, because feeling bad about something is to hypothesise you've done something wrong, I didn't want to think we'd done anything wrong. But I couldn't stop remembering it, so it seemed we must have. Instead, I thought how Anna had made me do it; she'd made me do so much. I felt slightly better every time I told myself that.

Inside, the park was the same as I remembered it. I looked at the map with the castle at the end, the rides, the right way to walk, the times the princesses and cartoon characters were appearing; that way it dictated our day.

In front of us a kid let go of its mouse-shaped balloon. As the giant pink foil ears floated away the kid started to cry. Adam ran back, whimpering himself as if it had been his balloon. Leo hugged him into his chest, saying over the top of his head, *They still let those be sold? Death trap for birds.* Anna laughed in her annoying way. *I'm being serious,* Leo said. *I know,* Anna said, *that's the problem.*

She walked on ahead of us, took her water out of her bag, drinking as she walked. I realised I was almost her height. I drew myself up to it, turned my head to Leo and tried her smile out on him; he smiled back at me. Adam ran between the two of us. It was kind of nice so long as I didn't think about the things he did.

How come you know her? Leo said. *Oh,* I said, *I babysit. I help sometimes after school when Anna's out. You're ever so enterprising, aren't you?* he said; I nodded as he began to frown. *Out where?* he said. *I don't know,* I said, *she's just out sometimes; maybe she needs a break. Yeah, maybe,* said Leo. *Her whole life's a break, though. I don't know,* I said. *Sometimes I think she's not OK; she is OK, isn't she?*

She – no, she – Leo said. *She's erratic. We had – well, something really tricky happened when we lived in the city, and I thought coming here would help; fresh start, I said to her, but yeah, it's not really changed anything. She's worse, if anything. I'm just trying to get through it. She'll come out the other side; people always do.*

I knew then he was a shit doctor. One who didn't really understand how complicated things could be. Probably one who thought pills would fix everything. I'd known enough like that. So had Mum. You could swallow all the medicine in the world; it never fixed anything for as long as everything else stayed the same.

I hope she does, I said. *You know she keeps calling me Ava? I told her I was Bethany but she's like Ava this, Ava that, sometimes Ada even, which is just weird.* I was watching him. His eyes flickered, but his face didn't change.

Does she? he said. *That's a concern.*

She does, I said, stroking his arm. *It's very disconcerting. Who's Ada?*

No one, he said. *She must have mistaken you for someone else.* But he said it quickly, stumbling over the words, the way I've learnt not to when I'm lying.

Adam grabbed Leo's sleeve. *Daddy,* he said, pulling him towards a simulator, all white and boxed in, *I love this one I love this one I love this one.*

You coming? Leo said, and we ran over to it. Anna came over slowly, her eyes invisible behind her dark glasses. It made her seem too far away. *You coming on?* Leo said to Anna, but she shook her head. *No, I think I'll sit this one out.*

She sat on the fake, overly green grass at the side of the simulator taking photos of us in the line for a while. When I checked my phone, she'd cropped Leo out, captioned Adam and me: *great day for a family day out*. Already there were comments: *Who's the girl?* and *Anna, your sister is so like you* and *Ada?!?!* and my favourite, *Holy f**k.*

Inside the simulator we sat down, strapped ourselves in as a filmed rollercoaster came on, and as it did, music began to come at us from all sides from numerous tiny speakers dotted along the top of the simulator, the drums getting more and more insistent, then even louder when they were joined by more after a few beats. The swooping sound of synths assaulted us from all directions. We were watching a film of the rollercoaster, as though we were inside a carriage on a rollercoaster and not the simulator. Most of the rides at the park were like this, saving on risk and insurance. The repetitive voice of the singer combined with the beat combined with the volume made me feel ill. I wanted to run away or throw up or both; black spots pricked at the back of my eyes; breathing hurt. I looked at Adam and Leo; they both had their hands in the air as we appeared to go down a steep drop. I tried to raise my arms, but they were heavy. Instead, I let them hang at my side. I shut my eyes, but the problem wasn't the film, it was the music – something was odd with the baseline; it was making my chest tight, as if it was also a memory, but not one I wanted to have.

Next to me Adam and Leo screamed sounds of pure, distilled pleasure so I knew they were having the time of their lives. Then it stopped as suddenly as it had begun and the door in the side of the machine opened, ejecting us into the scorching sunshine. I must have looked at the sun for too long because when I blinked I could see it in miniature but black. I blinked and blinked to try to make it go away but Anna was there on the grass, her long legs out in front of her, still snapping away at us.

Worried I'd faint, I held onto Leo's arm; he put it around me to steady me as we walked across to Anna. Leo said, *She doesn't feel good,* to her. She smiled at me. *Would some of my water help?* she asked. I swear she tried to wink. I took it from her, drank it, trying not to show how much it burnt my throat.

ANNA

Ava didn't look well when she came off the rollercoaster, flushed almost. Leo was holding her up, his hand on the small of her back. All I could see was that; his hand, her back. He steered her towards me. *She doesn't feel too good,* he said, *she's going to sit the next one out.*

I thought I saw the faintest trail of white across the bluest sky; maybe my eyes were making it up. I sat with my head tilted looking up at it, so I didn't have to look at them.

You don't need to go on it, I said to Ava, *the boys can go,* but Ava said no, she was fine, she didn't want to spoil it for anyone. *Give her some of your water,* Leo said. I gave her my bottle and watched her eyes widen as she gulped it.

As we walked towards Adam's favourite ride, someone in a giant dog costume – supposed to be the famous cartoon dog but a shitty replica – came lumbering over to him, its oversized head shaking from side to side, dragging its tail in its wake. Adam stopped and stared as it slowly came towards him. Adam's never liked teddy bears or soft toys – something about the feel of their fur; he said it made his teeth feel sick. I didn't know what he meant by that, but I kept quiet, which is often the best thing with Adam, otherwise he keeps trying to explain. I just smiled at him most of the time.

Somewhere deep inside the dog's costume was a sound button, because when it arrived in front of us it started to bark and pant. I think its eyes were part eyes, part speakers. Adam stood stock still, staring at the dog, which reached out its oversized, giant paw. Time was so muddled that the thing was both happening, and not happening and had already happened. There was nothing I could do but watch as the dog laid a synthetic arm on Adam. He shook. He yelled. He shook and yelled. The little fucking moron. Why he couldn't just be good like Ada, I didn't know.

Ava shooed the dog away and Leo took Adam by the shoulders and whispered things I couldn't hear until he was calm again. I felt better knowing he didn't really mind about the dog, he just liked to make it look like he was upset.

They looked so beautiful there, Leo with his head bent to Adam's and the light making halos in their hair; I knew I had to take a picture. I took my big camera out, adjusted the saturation just a little to make the colours richer. Looking through the screen at it, I knew it was the perfect shot. I'll schedule it for tomorrow, I thought, before walking over to where Adam and Leo were. Leo smiled at me, one of his rare open smiles, like he really was with us; something was putting him in a good mood. *You coming?* he said, jerking his head over to Adam's favourite ride, the one with the awful song. *I think I will sit this one out after all,* Ava said.

Sure, I said to Leo and the world stopped in that moment. All it contained was me, Leo and Adam. For a split second, they were all I wanted; they were enough; I felt light; if time could have stayed stopped, everything would have been fine; I could have kept loving them; I felt the thing in me that could only look instead of feel begin to break; I smiled at them both; it would all be OK, I could see that then, but time did what time always does; it started as we walked up the steps as Adam waved at Ava, shouting goodbye to her, smashing the crystalline moment.

I strapped myself into a giant pink teacup next to Adam; Leo grinned his lunatic grin across to me. *Hold on,* he said, and then the teacups began to spin as the ride started. The mechanism under the conveyor belt started groaning. I wondered, like I always did every time, if this would be the time it malfunctioned. We spun through the ride's entrance into the darkness, Leo turning the silver wheel in the middle to make it *faster faster faster* like Adam was shouting, eager, eager, eager. I hoped he wouldn't pee this time. The music started, the squeaky voices grating already. We rode past plastic caves and marooned fibreglass ships, past a tiny Mount Rushmore and a shrunken Eiffel Tower. I didn't know if we were meant to be in Paris or Vegas. Pisa's leaning tower was leaning more than it should, as if its collapse was imminent. I knew the song was in and under my skull, so much so that for the rest of the day I'd be singing it over and over in my head. I felt nauseous, utterly unmoored.

Leo's mouth was going up and down in the half-light, but the sound didn't reach me; he looked like one of the dummies in the displays, crashing their plastic cymbals close together. I nodded and smiled. He frowned. I shrugged, pointed to my ears. Adam was dancing with his arms above his head; I smiled at him, copying him, raising my hands above my own head, waving them around, and that moment was beautiful, me and him dancing together, until his arms started to jerk wildly. I still thought he was dancing until foam came from his mouth and his head fell forwards onto his chest.

Leo screamed; he shouted, *Where's the buzzer?* but sounded like he was under water. There was no buzzer. There was no way to stop the ride. Leo was next to Adam in full hero mode, clearing his airway, as the teacup spun more and more wildly. He was listening to his pulse. I was frozen, only able to watch as the music got louder and louder and louder and the teacup kept spinning until Leo shouted at me to turn the wheel to try to make it stop but I turned it the wrong way, making the cup spin faster until realising my error, I turned it the other way and it began to slow as the ride did too. Then we were out into the Day-Glo sunshine and the teacup stopped abruptly and the bar over our legs flung open and Leo lifted Adam out and carried him over to where Ada was, Adam's head rolling back up to the sky as around me all the children walking, holding their parents' hands, were you and you and you and you; the world was full of you; everywhere I looked there was only you at every age you'd ever been; Ada, you were there, you were everywhere that day, clutching balloons, laughing, skipping, running away from me in the same way you had all your life.

AVA

I thought Adam was dead when Leo brought him over to me. He seemed to be carrying him like an offering. I leapt up; *Is he OK?* I said. *What happened?* He didn't say anything.

Leo sat him down on the grass, opened Adam's little palm-tree-patterned shirt and put his ear to his chest, felt his forehead. All over his chest were tiny feather bruises. *What are these?* Leo said to Anna; she shook her head, kept her eyes wide and her mouth shut. I was ready to shrug if he looked at me. He didn't.

Frowning, Adam opened his eyes, asking in a baby voice where he was, looking around like he'd just been born. Leo kept asking him to do things, to walk in a straight line, to look up and down and from side to side, like he was a sea lion at the zoo. Leo declared he seemed to be OK, but maybe best to have him checked over at the GP on Monday. Anna nodded.

He crouched down and held Adam to his chest after he'd examined him. I wanted to make sure he was OK but Leo didn't move. *Do you want to go home?* he said. *Of course he does*, said Anna. *Shhh*, said Leo, *let him speak*. Adam looked at both of them. He was trying to choke back his tears the way you do when you're a kid. *I want to stay*, he said, *I don't want to ruin the day. Oh, you won't ruin it,* Leo said, staring at Anna.

Anna, give Adam your water, he said. Anna shook her head; *There's none left,* she said. I could see the fear in her eyes, like she was pinned up hard against a wall she couldn't back any further into. Just for fun, I thought I'd help her out. I said, *Anna, I hardly had any, there's loads left. I thought that,* said Leo. *What's wrong with you?*

Anna swallowed, handed her water over; Adam took a huge gulp of it before spraying it all over Leo, tiny pockmark explosions landing all over the front of his sage-green T-shirt. *It's not water*, he shouted. Leo took the water from Adam, shaking his head at Anna; *Tell me it's not,* he said, before taking a drink, and then he closed his eyes and bit his bottom lip hard. He stood with Anna's bottle in his hand, his body swaying a little, as if the wind was behind him and it wasn't the hottest day since records began.

ANNA and AVA

To begin with we thought we'd got away with it. We didn't look at each other as Leo lifted Adam's top and saw the bruises. Leo was too intent on keeping Adam alive to worry about them.

We exhaled too soon.

Adam needed water and we both knew what was in the bottle and it felt then like something buried was about to be uncovered. Afterwards, when Leo looked up, we knew it wasn't a game anymore.

At some point, one of us had stopped playing.

What happens when one person stops playing is, the one who's still having fun doesn't know how to stop. The anger intensifies when they have nothing left to lose. That's when you really need to be careful. That's when you really discover who you are playing with and how far they'll go to keep the game alive.

We looked at each other as the sun hit the highest point in the sky, making our shadows disappear; we could see it in each other's eyes, the way the light in them had stopped being soft and had turned to a hard, glinting thing, the set of one of our mouths more determined than it had been before and we each thought we knew, then, how it had to end.

ANNA

Leo looked at me, the world turned and I was on the ground, opening my eyes after a pause, and there were blanks there like snow is after sleet; round, widening holes, more and more space with nothing to fill it with. Leo and Ada were leaning over me, two circus clowns, their faces painted with concern.

I pushed the palms of my hands into my eyes so the world went black and then, when I pulled them away, there was a second's flash of pink where I was back in the womb. I liked that flash so I did it again and again and again and would have lain there all day just repeating it over and over and over, but they took an arm each and heaved me up just like we did that first day with the dog and Ada was Ava again, pulling me, hauling me, and I sat up, put my head between my knees and spat hard on the ground, just so I could feel like I was doing something.

Adam was shouting, *Mummy,* crying as he spoke. I turned to where he was, pulled him down and held him close, that first baby smell coming from the top of his warm head. I pulled him to me and sat back down on the ground, pulling him onto my knee. I nuzzled him in; the smell wasn't just his, it was Ada's too; after she wasn't strong enough to shower and she wouldn't let me sponge her down, the faintest smell used to escape from her head when I cradled her into me all the nights she couldn't sleep. I kept sniffing him over and over like a tom cat would a kitten they didn't trust, and it was then that the knowledge of how wrong I'd been became like the sun was when I pulled my hands away from my eyes, these bright flashes of how mistaken I'd been for so long. Adam wasn't the wrong baby, he'd been the right baby all the time, and here he was, my bruised and sick baby, the baby I'd never had enough heart to love, all long arms and legs, baby no longer, just a boy I couldn't remember seeing grow. Still smelling the hot summer scent of Adam, I looked up to where Ava was talking to Leo, twirling her hair round and round her finger as if she'd known him for longer than a day. She looked tarnished somehow, like her cheap coating had begun to wear off; she was nothing but a gaudy imitation of my daughter, my daughter, my baby, my baby I couldn't save and my other baby, heavy on my knee, covered with bruises we made on him; I heard the sound of Ava's laugh split into many pieces and the answering call of Leo's; what was it that amused them so much? How could she be here? How could I have let her in? All my terrible desire, all the things I had wanted and tried not no want; how they had eaten me and corroded me and worn me thin; I had never thought about the cost of any of it, ever; I had gone and gone and spun and turned and never cared to ask; I had been a mass of want and want and want and now this thing I had invited into our lives cared not who she threw to the wolves or how she did it; I could feel everything I'd drunk make its way out of my stomach and onto the melting tarmac and I heaved and heaved and heaved and longed to be free of the weight of the two of them, but to keep my Adam; all I wanted was to wrap him up and run away from them both. But that wouldn't have kept him safe. I was always the last thing anyone needed.

AVA

Just when I thought I was done with Anna, she went and fainted. She lay, crumpled there like a baby lamb. She really was good at getting attention. I helped Leo pull her up and Anna sat there, stalling for time with her head on her knees.

She did a good act, sitting there slouching; she grabbed Adam as an extra prop, which really added to the scene. I looked at Leo and could see he was almost convinced by her. He was such a fool; he'd forgive her anything. I knew I had to do something some might call drastic. Especially after she threw up to add to the overall effect.

After she was sick, I threw myself to the ground next to her, I put my arms around her and whispered into her ear, *You fucking light borrower.* Then I started to rub her back. She stared at me, unable to understand what I'd just said. She was a stupid woman, all for show. Tears had made a mess of her face. Her eyes were red and puffy. Up close in the hard sunlight, she looked old. I could see the lines at the edges of her eyes. All the things she'd taken care to disguise or I'd tried not to notice were suddenly so obvious. She looked old enough to be my mother.

She *was* old enough to be my mother.

Thinking of that made me feel a little bit sick, and I thought I was the one doing the stringing along. Although she looked old, she also looked like a strange, helpless kid sitting there. I knew she was doing it deliberately. All Leo would see was how vulnerable she looked. I could see her sniffing Adam's head; it was so obvious that she was thinking something trite like how much she needed him or that she'd remembered she loved him. I couldn't stand predictable people.

I knew she'd kick me out. I knew it was done. I felt a white stab of jealousy. I didn't want her, but I wanted her to still want me. It was clear now, she didn't. Leo was looking at her like he loved her again.

I wanted to pull my hair out carefully at the roots like I'd seen Anna do sometimes. She thought I didn't notice when she ran her hand up under the top layer of hair, quickly yanking one out. I wanted to throw something. I wanted to shout. Watching her sitting on the ground, I knew whatever I did next, I needed to make the right move. I couldn't have a visible tantrum, no matter how badly I wanted to. I needed to do something to get them both back. It was vital that I thought it through quickly.

I sat down next to Anna, smiling at her, so she wouldn't know what it was I was thinking. I made sure I looked at her like I had always looked at her, but softer even than that. I wasn't letting them get away with doing this to me. I needed to make the last couple of weeks worth something. I wasn't letting them both let me go without there being consequences; I needed them to remember me. I like that about myself. I'm memorable. Other people, they're so good at being victims. Not me. Whatever happens, I would be victorious. I like winning.

I was leaving in the morning. It wasn't like I'd have to see their sad little faces again. Even in my dreams I wouldn't let them come back to me.

With nothing to lose, I began to rub her back. I put my finger on her ankle, circling round and round the bone, ran it slowly up her legs and around her hem. I did it lazily, slowly, looking up at Leo, who was staring at us. I unbuttoned the top of her dress, began to caress the bruises there, but not covering them, so Leo could see the obvious teeth marks on her skin. I bent towards her mouth and although I was repulsed by the smell of her vomit, I leant forwards and kissed her for as long as I could stand. She didn't do anything. Just sat, drunk and high and blinded by grief, blinking at me as if she didn't have a clue who I was.

Then I leant across to Adam and ruffled his hair, telling him he was so cute. I stood up, raised my eyebrows and smiled at Leo. Anna staggered to her feet and stood next to me, looking at the ground. I knew she was tense, waiting for what was coming next.

Leo stood staring at me; he was smaller somehow, like the air had been let out of him. Anna looked more like a puppet than she ever had, hanging there, her head down but her shoulders high. *See,* I said to Leo, *you're not the only one I've been fucking.*

What the hell, Bethany? he said. *I don't understand.*

Then Anna whipped her head back so quickly I'm sure I heard it crack and she looked at me, no longer far away; it was her turn to say, *Bethany, what the actual fuck?*

ANNA

I didn't understand. Her words didn't make sense. She called me a light borrower, whatever that meant, then she said to Leo, *You're not the only one I've been fucking*, like there'd been something between us, and there was nothing, was there? Nothing. Just skin and sweat and salt and that was all. Only small, molecular things, not things to give words so harsh to.

Then Leo called her Bethany again, the same way he had in the house, and I stared at her, unable to know who she was: Ava, Ada, Bethany.

She had a wild look about her; all of Ada had left her face until there was no trace of my dead girl left; she was gone again. I wanted to howl, I wanted to ball my hand deep into a fist and hit Ava or whoever she was, over and over and over and over until she was nothing other than flesh, blood and pulp but I couldn't do that when I could hardly stand; things unspooled again like they had after the dog, and these were the things I saw: Adam, the mirror, the dress, us playing with him, Ava in my dresses, my dresses in the bin, teeth in my skin, Ada, this not Ava. I couldn't get the air I needed into my lungs; my ribs were tight and strangling me when *Bethany* escaped from my mouth in one strangled hiss; it felt like such a strange thing to be calling her. Her face didn't move; I wanted again to slap her, to make her do something; she was so empty, only a shell; I repeated it again; *Bethany*, I said; she smiled, nodded and said, *Exactly, I was never Ava or Ada; I was never yours.*

AVA

Leo wouldn't take us home. He said, *We are here for Adam, we will have a good day.* And that meant we went on rides and bought popcorn and threw it in the bin and Adam spun and smiled and Anna drank from her bottle and threw me looks across the top of it and I slipped her pills into my mouth, grinding them down until I didn't taste their bitter, hard edge; my mouth turned dry as the day and I didn't care for it or for any of them; I was counting down the hours to my deliverance.

There was something unmistakably wrong with the three of them. I'd been willing to give Leo the benefit of the doubt. I'd liked him in the woods. But there was something undone with him too, as if us staying at the park, going on the stupid rides, looking like we were some happy family, would fix everything. Suddenly he seemed more broken than Anna, more ground down somehow; there were just flashes of it as we walked, small indicators, he'd sigh or wipe his forehead or grind his teeth, squeaking them tightly together until a high-pitched squeal escaped into the summer air. He kept sniffing too, loudly, looking at me to see if I'd registered. The sniffing was the worst part.

ANNA

The clouds were rolling in, blocking the sun; we were cold for the first time in weeks. Eventually Adam said he wanted to go home.

My body did things, but I wasn't in it. I don't know when I was last properly inside myself. Having kids will do that to you. When they come out you expel a piece of yourself into the world, and it is as if you lose yourself. You can't stay in your body after you have them; it's no longer yours but theirs; they demand that of you and if you don't give them that then there's something wrong with you and all the other mums, the ones with the straight hair and the perfect jeans, the ones I looked like but never really was, they'll lynch you; mothers, they're a fucking lynch mob; better do as they say and think and demand, otherwise they're after you.

My body that hadn't been mine since Ada or Adam or Ava or Leo even, or before, or ever, was safely far away, the way I liked it best.

I sat in the car with my eyes shut, Leo behind the wheel. He kept making a sniffing sound now we were in the car. I couldn't stand it; I reached under the seat and pulled out the paper bag with the emergency pills in it and shook some into my hand. *Forfuckssake*, he said; at least he stopped sniffing for a second. *Those too?* Ava laughed from the backseat. *Naughty Anna*, she said. *Fuck you, Bellamy,* I said and then I started to laugh and Ava and I were laughing like the world was about to end, because it already had; we couldn't get the breath into our lungs and Leo and Adam were both sniffing again, making the air thick and tight as it clung to us; how we managed to breathe, I don't know; it was too much, stupid fuckers, all of us. I thought briefly of taking the wheel and turning it into the oncoming traffic moving away from The Spit, into the few cars going in the opposite direction with their lights on, as out to sea the sky turned a deeper and deeper grey until long, black tendrils reached into the water.

Look, look, look, shouted Adam from the backseat, suddenly excited again, *the Heat Death is coming, do you see it?* He started to clap his hands together. *I'm not sure it's not already been,* Leo said, thinking he was being smart. Bethany giggled, impressed.

It would have been so easy, one sharp, hard turn. We'd gone so far already, one more thing would have been nothing, but I didn't. Leo turned the climacontrol up and up and up until my teeth chattered.

I shut my eyes because it didn't matter anymore; IT had happened, The End had come. I didn't need to worry anymore about invasions or erosions; it didn't matter if it had come with fireworks, The Wave or just damp, rolling clouds; what mattered was that it finally had come; something had happened and something was done.

That was enough.

I shut my eyes.

AVA

When Anna slumped in her seat, I thought I should say something to Leo. Mostly because I was freezing. I needed him to turn the stupid cooler off. *I'm cold*, I said. *Would you mind?*

Sorry, he said, *didn't catch that.*

I shouted at him over the sound of it; *I'm sorry, yeah, I shouldn't have done that.*

He switched it off.

Yes, he said, *you shouldn't.*

It was just fun to begin with, I said, *I don't know. She was just there.*

Was it – he said. *Did she pay you?*

I said, *No, she didn't.*

Why do it then? he said. *You're quite driven by money.*

That bit hurt.

I am not, I said.

You charged me, he said, *even when we didn't . . . you know.*

It's OK, I said, *you can say fuck. Adam's sleeping.*

Adam was lying there with his chin on his chest like only kids can do and he had drool coming out of his mouth, soaking his shirt, making the palm trees wetter and darker.

I think it's fair enough, I said, *to charge. I was delivering a service. That's how it works.*

He looked at me in the rear-view mirror.

You really are dead inside, he said.

Fuck you, I said. *You paid to fuck me. I'm basically a kid. A kid who looks like your dead daughter. Don't you see how fucking creepy that is? At least Anna knew it was weird.*

He shook his head.

You don't look like her, he said. *You don't even come close. Anna's ill, she sees her everywhere. She dresses up as her. She's obsessed. It wasn't about you; you were just there.*

I stopped listening to him. We were on the road leading to The Spit. News crews had built towers looking over to the sea, their equipment covered by thick tarpaulin. The sky was black, the air heavy; my head hurt. It was just beginning to rain, small spit marks on the window. There was a queue of cars tailing back.

Just drop me here, I said, *I'll be quicker walking.*

Sure, he said.

I was just about to slam the car door when he said, *One thing.* I put my head back in. *Yeah?* I said. *The Ava bit,* he said, *was that you or Anna? I need to know. Oh,* I said, *that, that was pure Anna. You're right, she's mental.*

I slammed the door as hard as I could; through the glass, Adam's head jolting back as he woke.

ANNA

The first time I woke that night I was in bed. I don't know how I got there. My tongue was stuck to the roof of my mouth. I was naked on top of the covers. The rain was flinging itself against the window.

My head beat its own rhythm.

I stretched out to check Leo wasn't there. I shut my eyes to make sleep instead of memories come.

I remembered coming home, him pushing me up against the wall, my pants around my feet, the tips of his fingers, hard and calloused, looking at me as he did it, staring right at me; his eyes were a hard, transparent blue. Then I knew that something had switched; he'd shifted tense and position, from wondering what I would do, to knowing what he was going to do. It didn't matter what I said or did; he was leaving anyway. What I said next, when I filled in all the blanks for him, didn't really make any difference. It made me feel lighter at least. The abluting power of confession.

AVA

I could've made a fortune as I walked home that night. So many Watchers, mostly men, sitting in their deckchairs drinking from their bottles and cans. The more professional ones had on their full fishing gear. I thought about what it would be like if The Wave did come, how the fish would rain down on their pathetic heads and they'd call it an omen or something stupid. The news would love it; they'd talk about it for weeks, months maybe, until the next one. However long that wasn't. The rest of them – the opportunists, the bored, the drifters, the displaced, the misplaced – they had thick black bin bags over their heads.

They put so much effort into keeping dry, but they were here to watch a fucking wave. Some people. Sometimes, in crowds, I'd try to get some business, but I wasn't in the mood.

I walked on to the horseshoe of cottages at the village green.

When I'd driven past them with Anna, she'd called them quaint. I'd nodded. I didn't tell her about damp or the mice or the paper-thin walls we could hear the neighbours through, and the neighbours being able to do the same to us. I could smell the bins from the bottom of the garden; the binmen had been on strike all summer – said it was too warm to work for so little pay. It didn't matter at Anna's house, with its own disposal system, but it was beginning to stink in the village. The path was littered with rubbish from the foxes ripping open the bags next to the bin.

At least I didn't need to feel guilty for not cutting the brown grass; it was so long it bowed over. It was better to leave it long in the heat – wouldn't burn that way.

I pushed the door open; Mum never locked it – said we had nothing worth stealing. She was right. From the sitting room came the sound of sirens on the TV. The hallway still smelt damp; I guessed Mum hadn't managed to fix the leak under the sink.

I took my shoes off, but walking along the spongey carpet, it wasn't long before my feet were damp. I shouted, *Hello,* but Mum didn't answer. In the sitting room she was sleeping in her chair, a full ashtray next to her. I picked it up, heavy cut crystal in my hands, wondering where it had come from and how much she'd get for it. I guessed soon she'd need to think about selling things. I moved as quietly as I could through the bead curtain separating the kitchen from the sitting room.

I decided to try to fix the leak for her; I needed one less thing to worry about. I lay on my back, my phone torch at my side, lying under the u-bend in the sink. The online tutorial made it look easy when it wasn't. It wasn't long before I gave up. It wasn't like I couldn't leave her money to pay for it.

I went into the sitting room and switched off the TV; it was too loud for her to sleep through it all night. I sat on the edge of the sofa, watching her sleep. Her face was beginning to fall in on itself in ways Anna's wasn't. There were pictures on The Screen of Anna's fortieth, of gold balloons in a 4-0, a three-tiered cake and two nights at a spa with 'the girls'. *Thank God for the hubster,* the caption said.

It was stupid, but I suddenly felt a small amount of affection for the house. I'd never liked it, but it felt weird knowing this was final. I'd thought about how it would feel for so long, had pictured myself running away down the path and never looking back. But it wasn't like that. Here was my home scar. I knew I had to be one of the limpets who learnt to adapt; that's the problem with not having anyone to look after you: it's adapt or die. Sometimes it got a bit tiring. I looked at the sitting room, wished I'd been able to make it be enough for me, or that Mum could've made it safe for us. Some things are too much to expect from one person.

My nose began to tickle. I knew I was going to cry. I took a tissue from the teak unit Mum had found abandoned on the street. She loved it; I hated it. I took a pen from the top drawer, found some loose paper and put it against the wall, knowing Mum would go mad if I scratched her precious unit. I wanted to write something eloquent, but I'd never been great with words. I crumpled the first sheet into a ball, dropped it on the floor. It was better to leave it blank; there was too much and too little to say. I would have left it at that, but it felt important to try to get the sink fixed. She couldn't keep living with the smell. I took another piece of paper and I wrote, *Mum, you need to remember to get the sink fixed. Here's some money for it. Or you can use it to go away until you fix the Meter situation. I'm at Dad's for a bit. Don't worry about me. Beth. x*

It didn't sound too bad. I walked over to the pole in the middle of the room, wrapped my legs around it, had one last time sliding down it. Mum hardly used it anymore. It had been one of her madder ideas, back when she thought about being self-employed. It had its benefits, though; I doubt I'd have come up with my business idea without it.

SUNDAY

ANNA

I slept the sleep of the dead after that, the way that happens when something's ended. When I woke for the second time I did so in a panic, the house still and Leo still not there. I knew something had happened, but what, I couldn't remember.

I fell back into a strange sleep filled with stranger-still dreams. I dreamt of Ada in the pram, of forgetting Leo's birthday, of being trapped in a lift in a department store trying to find him the perfect present, of bending down to wipe Ada's tears – she hated lifts – and her smiling at me, but it was Ava's smile. I screamed in the dream to wake myself up. It used to work but for the last couple of weeks life had taken on the texture of unreality to such a degree, I could no longer wake myself from a dream, the distinction between waking and sleeping having switched.

Morning came sharp and loud with the sounds of swifts at their nest. I thought about Leo and how excited he'd be, before yesterday started to come back in the wrong order but enough to know why the bed was empty and his den too, and why he wasn't in the garden when I went out, the smell of the fresh rain thick and heavy the way the air had been the day before, the lilac and honeysuckle sweet and overpowering in my nostrils, the lavender too. The worst sky I'd ever seen out over the sea, blood-red fingers spreading towards The Spit, and where was he? The car was there but he was gone; I didn't care about my wet feet or the grass I took back into the house as I ran up the stairs to where Adam was sleeping on his back with his mouth open and his nose in the air and, fuck, I couldn't remember if I'd put him somewhere – had I done something to him? I checked the knife rack, I checked the freezer, the bathroom, the en-suite, the wardrobe, under the sofa, and just as I was thinking of the chest freezer in the outhouse I saw the space by the door where his shoes should be. His brand-new shoes that had come in the gunmetal-grey box with white writing that said: *VOID: Race the Darkness*; I'd joked that perhaps they were making a bold claim, but he hadn't laughed, just said, *They're made from coconut leaves*. Or something like that. The shoes were gone; the door wasn't locked. I slipped my walking boots on, took my oilskin from the utility room and went out into the rain; drips of it were rolling down my neck and breaking on my coat and they were hitting my face as I ran shouting his name; the sky lowered as I ran into the woods in the direction I'd seen Ava coming from so often, the branches cracking, my feet catching on the roots as I ran, the smell of damp overlaying everything. The smell came as a relief, meaning, as it did, that the heat had broken and we were back to *normal*, but even as I was running, I knew that wasn't true; I was shouting his name over and over as I ran deeper and deeper into the woods where it was darker and darker, becoming darker still, overheard the sound of many birds screeching as they flew in from the sea; the trees hid the sight of them; only the sound made its way to me. I kept shouting, louder and louder for him, until my throat was raw, my voice weakening. I ran past the tree they called The Way Tree, the one they hung bells from, its branches pointing to the ground as if in sorrow or submission, bells surrounding it, ribbons shredded in the mud; I smelt the green algae rising from the pond and there he was, lying against a crumbling old shed, a faint print of where his body had once leant against it on the fading blue paint; he was just lying folded up and in on himself; he was wearing the same clothes he had been the day before; at his side were my secret pills – the bottle was empty just as the bottle of whisky he'd taken from the snug was; I was kneeling down next to him; I was wiping away the webs covering him as I was trying to look at the sky but all that was above me was a tangle of leaves and I was yelling long and hard; I was hollering and hollering as if it would be an incantation enough: *Ada*, I screamed, *Ada, Ada, Ada, Ada, Ada, Ada*, and I was crying then; for the first time since you left I could cry. I could cry. I laughed because I was crying. I was human again, made of flesh and tears. I was laughing with relief. Finally, human in the middle of the woods, I felt for his pulse. I couldn't find it at first but then it was there, the faintest push against my finger. At least I think it was. It might have been the echo of my own heart rushing blood to my fingertips that I felt.

I thought about getting help. I really did. I thought about calling the ambulance. I thought about how blocked the road was and I thought about The Watchers and the red over the sea and I thought about how long it would take for them to get here and how little we had left on our Value Meter, but most of all, I thought about Adam and how he slept like a baby despite all that I'd done to him; I thought about his smell and how I'd got it wrong – they never had swapped my baby, it had been him all along; and good God, he was part of her too; he was more Ada than anything else, more than anyone I'd ever find again, and I needed to look after him, needed to finally think of him. I thought of the sight and sound of sirens and how frightening that could be for him. He'd have to see them and hear them, and it was easier for him not to have that; best to have a daddy just gone, a daddy not there anymore; I would make sure that when I did find Leo's body, I would find it on a school day, just after I dropped Adam off, and that would be perfect, yes, that was the best solution, I thought, as I scratched my fading bite marks.

I needed someone to talk to. Not Ava. I needed to hear the sound of my own voice. I needed it to sound authoritative. I felt unmoored, so much so I needed to be someone who knew things. I knew the journalists were waiting at the top of The Hill. I knew they'd love me to visit them, to say something clever. I could give them an insight into how it felt now it was raining, now the weather was feeling ominous. That's exactly what I'd call it, I thought, as I walked back to the car and drove away from The Spit, knowing Adam wouldn't wake when I was gone. I'd be home in time for breakfast.

ANNA and AVA

That was what happened, from the first day to the last. More or less.

We didn't mean it to be like that. It just is what it is. The way things are. They happen; life unravels; it's just one mistake, then a series of missteps. People like to call it choice, to make it sound like we aren't just part of one long accident.

What happened next, that didn't have anything to do with us. That's what the government said later when the inquiry came, washed their hands of it and all the Valueless people on The Spit. If they could, so can we.

This last bit, we are calling it an act of God.

PART III
WHOM GOD PRESERVES

> Time in the sea eats its own tail, thrives,
> casts these
> Indigestibles, the spurs of purposes
> That failed far from the surface.
> – Ted Hughes

4 | THE WAVE

It bears no relation to any reality whatever.
— Jean Baudrillard

AVA

After I wrote the letter, it made sense to leave. No point in hanging around places you're done with.

I lay on my stomach feeling my hipbones dig into the hard wooden floorboards as I pulled my tin of money out from under the bed. It was heavier than I thought it would be. I knew it was enough to last a while, if I was careful. And I am careful.

Anna, for all the way she looked so perfectly put together, was sloppy. She didn't notice if things went missing. I thought I'd try it out to see, just something small to begin with – earrings are so easy to lose after all. And necklaces are easy to slip into pockets and dresses fold down small and jumpers can be worn leaving houses if the person inside is, say, passed out on the sofa.

Little by little, I siphoned things away, knowing I'd need them when the time came, and there wasn't a better time, not really, than then. I packed all her things, leaving all of mine, apart from the jeans I changed into. I put one of her cashmere jumpers on without anything under it. It was so soft against my skin. I'd taken some books as keepsakes as well, short stories mostly. Adam had clearly read some of them too. Poor fucker.

I packed the bags of things I'd collected from people. I left all the diaries I'd written when I was really ill. Maybe they'd help Mum understand it a bit better. Maybe then she'd see I wasn't being difficult like she thought I was. How hard it was to be so hungry for the world but to be born to live a life that had nothing you wanted in it. She thought I wasn't hungry when, really, I was full of desire. The only way to tame it was to starve it, to make it bow before me. Until Mum came for it and the doctors too, with their solutions, answers, helpful suggestions. They didn't know what they were playing with, trying to make me better, didn't know what monster they might wake. Stupid fuckers. Every last one of them. I wanted her to read those diaries. I wanted her to finally know who she had as a daughter.

I put the bells I'd collected from The Way Tree in last. I thought I might need them in the future to keep in my pocket, for the anxious days, in case they started to come again.

It was hunger that brought me to Anna. I liked Anna as soon as I saw her. I liked her photos; even though they were pretty ridiculous, there was something nice about them. Her life in the city looked so different to anything I could have imagined, like something I'd seen in a film. I couldn't work out why she'd want to trade so much for so little. When I scrolled further back and saw pictures of Ada with broken hearts posted under them, rows and rows of black hearts, pink broken hearts, some white ones thrown in, I knew something had happened, although not what. Anna's How to Live When You're Swallowed by Grief course made it pretty clear.

The more I looked at Ada in the later pictures the more I saw how similar we both were. Not so much because our features were the same but because our hunger had made our faces and bodies the same shape. I looked at the photos of their house, their beautiful raw polished wood, the heavy patterned rugs, the textured cups; I knew I'd like it – there was always something to feel, to caress and to look at. Although, in the new house, Anna had made sure everything was flat, clean, soulless.

It was around that time I used to watch the films of Ada talking, with my phone propped at the side of the mirror, practising her movements until they were just about perfect. It wasn't as if I really thought out what I was going to do, but looking back, it began to look like I had.

I packed and walked down the stairs on the balls of my feet and closed the door softly behind me. I was leaving. I started to giggle; it seemed wild that I was finally doing it.

The village had a buzz to it that evening. The Watchers were in a festive mood – some had strung lights between the trees and set up speakers, music was blaring, people were dancing. It was the most alive I'd seen it in years. I waved to them as I passed; I liked the feel of it.

I walked along The Spit for one last time. I thought I saw him at the edge of the woods, his silhouette moving into the trees. I could have been wrong; there were so many strangers around; more than likely it was just a Watcher.

At the top of The Hill, the bus drew up; I looked out over the sea. The wind was picking up; it seemed disturbed. I climbed on the near-empty bus, flashed my Exemption Certificate. The seat was cold when I sat down; I stood up and put my jacket down to sit on it. Hardly anyone was travelling in the same direction as us; instead, the traffic coming towards The Spit was dense, everyone infected with the same excitement.

Lights woke me when we drove through the city centre. It didn't seem possible that I was there. I couldn't make it real. I pinched myself the way I usually did to try to feel something. It didn't work. Maybe I was so used to Anna's pills. I don't know. I began to scratch my upper arm, high enough for no one to see, low enough for it to be just in reach. Too quickly the city began to thin out into suburbs where rows of identical two-storey white houses with cars in their drives and soft light in the windows sat. I was almost glad I didn't live somewhere like that.

Then vacant office blocks, temples to late capitalism, I repeated, having read it somewhere, rolling the sound around my mouth. I also had in my bag, besides the short stories, a notebook of phrases I liked; I'd been keeping it for a while, collecting phrases from clients, and their wives sometimes too. Everyone on The Spit was so fucking lonely, it was its own disease.

The airport glowed, becoming a burnished sun on the horizon. It was quiet at that time of night. Most of the carbon protestors outside were sleeping, tucked safely inside their polyester tents. I checked in electronically, standing stock still as they scanned my bag. I expected the scanner to go off, but it didn't, then I went to the gate and stretched on the tartan-patterned seats as my eyes closed.

It was done.

WE

It was morning when the boy woke; the rain made it difficult to tell if it was night or day; the silence compounded the difficulty – where there should have been the sounds of morning, the mother making breakfast or the daddy in the shower, besides the sound of the rain, heavy on the skylight, there was only thick silence, a glowering silence he turned on his side to escape, pulling his pillow over his head to make it go away, but even then, it crept under, until the boy jumped up, screaming to break it, leaping out from under his covers, bounding across the floor in two leaps to switch his overhead light on; for a moment he sank back against the door as if in relief, but the light, he quickly realised, did little to help with the silence or the growing knowledge that he was alone in the house, otherwise how to explain the absence of any sound; he was against the door when he saw it on the opposite wall, a single white moth, speckled with black, its wings folded against its side; he moved towards it; he was all stealth as he did so, a boy on the hunt; it stayed where it was until he was nearly upon it, but then he noticed another below it and also to the right one with the same markings, its wings tucked in in the same way; he wanted to scream but knew he would disturb the moth; he would have liked to run away but his compulsion was pulling him closer, closer; as he drew nearer he saw there were not three moths but many, the wall covered with them, the air thick and full of them; they flew, circled, surrounded, him, obscuring the room; there were clouds and clouds of moths; when the boy opened his mouth to scream, a moth landed in there; he tried to spit it out but it was stuck; he put his hand into his mouth, peeling its wings from his tongue, his other hand fending the moths off his face, but there were too many; he knew then it was a bad idea to bring cocoons into the house just as We knew it was, this poor boy, so lacking in foresight, just like the rest of them; he shut his mouth, put his head down, ran to the bedroom door, slammed it shut behind him, hoping to keep the moths in, but of course it was too late; there were already moths in the hallway; he ran down the stairs making his feet heavy on every step, worrying about the ghosts he knew lived in the walls of the house, ghosts he believed were angered by his mother, ghosts he knew were at peace with him although he knew not why, there were things the boy knew that he couldn't explain; the rain continued to bounce off the skylight, making too much of a noise for the boy; he ran into the snug hoping to avoid the echoes ringing through the whole house, he ran into the kitchen, thinking of cereal with jam, of pink milk, his disaster movie turned up loud, then he was stopped by the sight out of the kitchen window: something was wrong with the sea.

AVA

I was first in line for boarding, right up the front of the tiny queue. On the plane, I was sitting at the window, my face looking out over the wet tarmac as morning ripped the sky open, when someone sat themselves down at the end of the row. I kept my eyes fixed on outside until they announced take-off and then I took my book from the pocket of the seat in front of me. I looked at the passenger out of the side of my eye, saw that he couldn't be that old, his skin still tight along his jaw, and his nose was turned up just the right amount at the end, his hair growing back off his forehead. I guessed the flight might be OK after all.

I thought if I didn't look up from my book at least I'd be reading something of Anna's when the plane exploded, but it wasn't like that. The plane accelerated, taking off more suddenly than I expected, fighting and juddering to break through the clouds, and I kept my eyes right on the book the whole time but suddenly there was sunshine and blue sky and I'd never even thought about how it might look up there with clouds below me. It was as if I'd escaped the weight of something I hadn't noticed until then. Something happened to my stomach; some pure raw feeling that didn't have a name arrived. It growled. I was hungry again.

Good choice, he said from the end of the aisle, looking at Anna's book. When I turned to him, everything inside the plane was lit differently, all white and fresh. *Have you read the unedited ones?* he said. I didn't have a fucking clue what he meant, so I said, *Not yet, no, next on my list, though.*

Tell me about it, he said. *Always so much to read, isn't there?* I said, *There really is,* thinking of the bare sitting room at home, and how Mum said books were too expensive, which hadn't mattered too much, until the library van stopped coming round. The seatbelt sign went off and he said, *Thank fuck,* and undid his and moved to the seat next to mine. When the drinks trolley came round I nodded when he asked if I wanted one.

He liked to talk. A lot. He was still talking when I looked out of the window over the Arctic Circle. *Bit of a geological artefact, still calling it that, don't you think?* he said. *I do,* I said, *absolutely.*

Sometimes, he said, *I think we should get rid of the old idioms, look to the future.*

Only a fool would think about the future, but I said, *Completely.* I said, *It's essential, isn't it, in the brave new world? Wow,* he said, *you're so switched on.* It never failed to amaze me how good I was at taking people in. He said, *Where is it you're going? Oh,* I said, thinking quickly, *I summer with my dad.*

Really? he said. *That's some Exemption. I know,* I said, *I'm lucky. My dad, well, he's a bit of a big deal, actually* –

I get that, he said, *I'm the same; not my dad, me.* He raised his brows and rolled his eyes in the most amazing way. Most people love any excuse to talk about themselves; all I needed to do was create the right circumstances. Seeing him do that with his eyes nearly made me spit my third gin out; instead, I made my eyes bigger. *Oh really?* I said, crossing my legs towards him and leaning a little bit closer. *Tell me more.*

Fuck. That was a mistake. He told me more and more and more and more. He had this immense capacity to talk until he was a dog at the races, going round and round and round. It was great for me; I hate questions. As he was talking to me, I nodded and smiled and drank and gave him big eyes and wound my hair round my fingers, made interested faces and encouraging noises; all the things I'd practised for years were coming in handy. Sometimes, I'd just touch his leg ever so lightly with my fingertips as he told me about his hot-shot job in green energy where the last of the big bucks were. He droned on about how all the regulations could be circumnavigated if you knew the right people and on and on and his suits were all hand-made in Italy it so happened. I ran my finger round the top of my glass when eventually he said, *So sorry, I've absolutely hogged the conversation, and there was me thinking I was a gentleman. How about you?*

Oh, I said, *there's not much to say, really.* I knew he'd like that – they always do; he'd probably call me enigmatic soon. I opened my mouth, shook my head a little bit and looked up as I breathed out, coughing faintly. It bought me time. *So, yeah, hard to know where to begin,* I said. *I'm doing literature, and* – I sort of glanced at the book and looked self-deprecating like the girls on the shows on TV.

My dad has a summer house in South Carolina, I said, knowing this guy was the type to holiday in the Hamptons, and I didn't want to be rumbled right at the start. *And an apartment in New York, obviously,* I said. I was getting dizzy from rolling my eyes so much so I sucked in my cheeks so he knew how bored the New York apartment made me. *And that's it, really,* I said. And then I paused, but he didn't say anything; shit, maybe he was interested. Just to fill in the silence, I said, suddenly inspired, *I have a shoot next week.* He leaned in even closer then; *I knew it,* he said, an air of supreme victory in his voice, *you're a model, of course you are, you dark horse.* I drew my left shoulder up to my chin to make sure I looked nonchalant. *Clothes horse more like*, I said, raising my eyebrows and making my eyes bigger at the same time in a way I didn't know I could but needed to catalogue for another time.

When the Hudson came into view, I could see all the places that, until then, had only existed on a map spread out on my bedroom floor. I had to remember to act like this was something I'd seen often; it wasn't anything special. *I get a bit nervous during landing*, I said, looking out of the window at the river with its islands and inlets; wherever I went, I decided, it had to be near the coast. The water was still and gentle as the trails of clouds cleared.

I could hold your hand, if you like, he said. *To be honest, I get nervous too.*

Aren't you cute? I giggled as he sat his wet palm in mine, hardly gripping my hand properly. I stared out of the window and thought how it had all been worth it, just to get here.

WE

Alone in the kitchen the boy knew for once and for all that The Wave was more theory than fact when what he saw coming towards him was not so much a wave but a shelf of sand, sea and sediment; the boy stood, transfixed by the sight of the seabed coming at him at such a pace, able only to watch, unable to scream or to run; learning for the first time, the last time, that time made no sense, that it could stretch and contract all in the same moment; as it came towards him he was no longer there but elsewhere with the sister the day the ants came; a great flying swarm of them invading the house in the middle of the summer, with wings the boy didn't know they had, this surprise defying all his ideas up until then of nature and the placid way it worked; they swarmed in all over the mother's cream carpet, up her cream curtains; the mummy opened windows and doors, ran at them with dusters and brooms, fly spray and insect killer; none of it was working and the sister was up the stairs in her bed where she was atrophying, day by day caught in a cannibal war of attrition; she was tired by then, knew it wouldn't be long, but she didn't mind; it was all she'd ever wanted after all, to be of a different use in the world; she knew all that would happen when it happened was that she'd switch places and finally be consumed and no longer endlessly consuming; a transition she'd been trying to dramatise for the mother and the daddy for so long, but the mother was not good at listening and the daddy not good at seeing anything other than pathologies and diseases, and this was how they came to frame her as sick, as mad, a thing to be fed instead of simply fed up. She felt the breeze coming from the open window, her lace curtains barely moving in it, but it was cold enough for her and her failing organs while downstairs the pest-control man taped up the sitting-room windows and doors, trapping the fumes in; of course it's safe, he said to the mother, it's not like we're ants, is it; he laughed as he strapped his plastic container to his back, releasing clouds of spray into the air, and the boy, frightened by the noise, ran up the stairs to where his sister had been gasping, rasping for breath, her lungs unable to fully inflate for the last time, and there she was, her lips blue and blueing; he took her hand and her nails were purple then, her hands too, and he climbed over her empty body, lay at her back and began to rub her fragile skin, the same as she'd done to him, all her protruding bones hurting his little fingers; as the water came towards him and time tumbled and tripped he was back there with the sister and the mummy gone away and the daddy too, and his eyes grew wide with amazement as glass splintered and crashed all around him and over the noise of it all he didn't hear the shrieking of birds the way they had been all morning, flying high above the woods, away from The Spit, knowing as they did how to escape what was coming; as the water broke The Watchers clapped and snapped, the news crews beamed real-time footage of The Wave's long-anticipated arrival from coast to coast before screens cut out, before footage was pieced carefully back together omitting the full scale of the disaster; the mother watched it happen from up on The Hill, speaking into microphones knowing it was already too late; all she could do was watch it happening just as she'd refused to see it coming, as the cameras captured pictures of where her house with the boy in it should have stood but instead there was nothing there, only water.

AVA

I said goodbye to him at baggage reclaim, telling him I only had hand luggage because most of my stuff was at my dad's house. *Of course,* he said, then he added, *Listen, can I get your number just to keep in touch? Sure,* I said, handing him my phone, *just put it in. I'll call you with mine.*

There you go, Anna, he said as he handed it back to me just as the alerts started to come through. It had happened when we were in the air, all the water, all the mess, all of it, right on my home screen; I looked up at the TVs at the side of the luggage carousel; they had the same breaking story blazing right out of the screens. He followed my eyes. *Holy shit,* he said, *that's awful.*

It is, I said. *Such a shame, especially since they literally saw it coming. Don't,* he said. *You can't say that.* I could tell he wanted to laugh, so I went just a tiny bit further to see how far I could push it with him; *Looks like a dump, though, doesn't it? Come on,* he said. *People have just died and we were only just up the coast; it's unbelievable.*

I stood, trying not to look too interested, but I was unable to stop staring. The Wave hit and hit and hit and was hitting again, obliterating all of The Spit, the village, the Sorting Centre, Mum. Then Anna was on the screen, just there, microphone to her mouth. She must've gone to give her opinion the way she was always doing, which meant she was safe, but Adam, Leo, where were they? Her face was frozen and shocked as she looked down towards the sea but only for a matter of seconds; it

245

was hardly even noticeable to anyone other than me before she collected herself and began to speak, her voice calm in the way only Anna could do. I'd been fine until then, but seeing everything I'd known ruined and gone, knowing it meant Mum was too, made me want Anna again. I knew I would spend the rest of my life with the want for her growing inside me; knew too that it was impossible ever to see her again; the only way I could keep her with me was to become her.

I fixed my eyes on the bottom of the screen so I didn't have to look at her, because if I hadn't, then I would have stood in the airport until the screens were switched off, just to see the clip of her. Rolling along the bottom of the screen it said: *Government refuses to assume responsibility for Human Collateral on The Spit, insisting only Low Value casualties.*

I need to use the toilet, I said. *I'll wait for you,* he said, *just to say bye properly. Sure,* I said. *Stay here.*

As I walked away, I saw my dad through the smoked-glass windows. He was standing there with his stupid ten-gallon hat making him about seven feet tall, his belly sticking out under his shirt where he tucked it into his loose chinos, the top four buttons of the shirt undone. Two girls were hanging off him, looking all excited, like little puppies. It was almost them that did it, but it wasn't; it was the sign he was holding, made from old cardboard with loads of felt-tipped flowers over it. Sometimes, it's just the little things that are too much. It all looked so sad, so eager; too eager, too sad. They didn't need to beg for me.

I was in the toilet when Anna's number flashed up on my screen; when I answered she didn't speak, just made a horrible sound of pain, a high-pitched note of loss nearly matching the cows in the dying summer night when their calves were taken.

I hung up, put the phone in the sanitary bin, pushing it down deep between other people's dried blood, and then I flushed, washed my hands and knew exactly what I was going to do next.

AFTER

The wind
Crosses the brown land, unheard.
The nymphs are departed.
				– T.S. Eliot

WE

Their end was only the beginning after The Wave came, bringing with it the Great Undoing; proceeding not in the way it had been prophesied, no horsemen, no signs in heaven, no mushroom clouds, no many-eyed wild beasts, just a prolonged demise; We watched, knowing there was no deliverance, no blood of the lamb, no Valhalla, no heaven, no hell, no nirvana, no boom of the end, no Heat Death like the boy wanted, not even fireworks; just us, watching, vain and inglorious, insistent on reclaiming our own territory; wars came, although by then they liked to call it conflict, softening the term a little; no one could stand to give things their proper names anymore; little boys, they'd trained their whole childhoods for this, learning to press buttons with their headsets on, tracking moving targets across the screen; murder is easy at a distance, preferably you don't have to get your hands dirty; one button pressed, enemy neutralised; they didn't even need to call them dead; just as the sea came in Waves, we watched people coming in the same way, displaced by heat, famine, conflict; they fought over the silliest things – water and wheat; some things never seemed to change, a constancy in their bickering at least; We watched as all the ideas they'd paid lip service to – tolerance, liberty, freedom – fell by the wayside; things, we knew, never changed, just came in cycles, history only a circle; We'd had enough of it and them, their meaningless borders, their flimsy flags, their insular ways, their touching belief that a beautiful life would be enough to insulate them from the horror of life; and so We came for them; as they went, life returned; cracks in concrete widening as trees broke through, all the once-living things trapped here under The Spit made use of in new ways, becoming oil, mulch, fresh earth, fossils for new organisms to find and wonder at; We do not miss them – it is impossible to miss what you never fully understood; it is only a relief, to feel this peace, for the air to be empty of their voices, filled only with the eternal sound of the wind blowing across the surface of the sea.

ACKNOWLEDGEMENTS

It feels disingenuous that it's only my name on the front of this book when so many debts of love and gratitude were incurred in the making of it; endless thanks to the following:

Matthew Marland, my agent at RCW, for never insisting I take the easy career route.

My editor, Lee Brackstone, for taking the necessary risks and emboldening me to do the same.

Ellie Freedman, for early championing and subsequent ideas.

For further editorial insights: Frances Rooney, Alice Graham and Sophie Nevrkla.

At Orion: Aoife Datta, Cait Davies, Lindsay Terrell and Tara Hiatt. Also Jenny Lord, Katie Espiner and Anna Valentine.

I can't write without listening to music. In this case, Lana Del Rey's *National Anthem* became the only song Ava would talk to me during, and if that sounds like voodoo, I think it was, a little. And to Andrew Weatherall's *End Times Sound* for bringing me back into the room and away from The Spit.

Rob Doyle for the early encouragement and reading. In the same spirit, Keiran Goddard.

For the necessary sustaining conversations: Lias Saoudi, Ewan Morrison, Darran Anderson, Jill Crawford, Dan Richards, Anna McDowell, David Keenan, Gavin Ritchie, Wendy Erskine, Joe Gibson and Kasimiira Kontio.

For keeping me alive, halfway fed and entertained all that strange long summer: Rebecca Palmer, Andrew Neale, Melissa

Hugel, Becky Thomas and Jon Gray.

For the gerbil story and the insistence that it *is all totally true*, along with the relish with which it was told: Juno and Tarn. For a different part: Euan.

To Nicola, for everything.

Finally, to my eldest daughter and her keen eye for the absurd, and to my three youngest children whose patience for my job far exceeds my own. I love you all, I'm sorry.

CREDITS

White Rabbit would like to thank everyone at Orion who worked on the publication of *Ava Anna Ada*.

Agent
Matthew Marland

Editor
Lee Brackstone

Copy-editor
Holly Kyte

Proofreader
Clare Wallis

Editorial Management
Frances Rooney
Alice Graham
Sophie Nevrkla
Jane Hughes
Charlie Panayiotou
Lucy Bilton
Claire Boyle

Audio
Paul Stark
Jake Alderson
Georgina Cutler

Contracts
Dan Herron
Ellie Bowker
Alyx Hurst

Design
Nick Shah
Joanna Ridley
Helen Ewing

Finance
Nick Gibson
Jasdip Nandra
Sue Baker
Tom Costello

Inventory
Jo Jacobs
Dan Stevens

Production
Sarah Cook
Katie Horrocks

Marketing
Cait Davies

Publicity
Aoife Datta

Sales
Jen Wilson
Victoria Laws
Esther Waters
Group Sales teams across
Digital, Field, International and
Non-Trade

Operations
Group Sales Operations team

Rights
Rebecca Folland
Alice Cottrell
Ruth Blakemore
Ayesha Kinley
Marie Hencke